A Fine Day
for Drool

Sharon Siamon

James Lorimer & Company, Publishers
Toronto, 1994

James Lorimer & Company Ltd. acknowledges with thanks
the support of the Canada Council, the Ontario Arts Council and the Ontario Publishing Centre in the development
of writing and publishing in Canada.

Cover art by Karen Harrison
Interior illustrations by Daniel Shelton

Canadian Cataloguing in Publication Data

Siamon, Sharon
  A fine day for drool

(A Lorimer blue kite adventure)
ISBN 1-55028-461-4 (bound) ISBN 1-55028-460-6 (pbk.)

I. Title. II. Series

  PS8587.I225F55 1994   jC813'.54   C94-931897-3
  PZ7.S53Fi 1994

James Lorimer & Company Ltd., Publishers
35 Britain Street
Toronto, Ontario M5A 1R7

Printed and bound in Canada

Contents

To Colin and Deb,
James and Finlay,
and Ajax, the cat.

With thanks to the group of young authors in
Pembroke who suggested great ideas for
A Fine Day for Drool *in the spring of 1994.*

1

Odie Joins the Enemy

"It isn't on any map!" Josie said, smugly. She tossed her dark head. "So you'll never find it, Kiff."

Kiff Kokatow fixed his teasing brown eyes on Josie's face. "Why do you care if I find Fort James?" he asked. "It's just an old trading post. It isn't worth anything."

"Not worth … " Josie spluttered. "That just shows what an ignorant person you are, Kiff Kokatow, as if I didn't know." She turned away and stormed out of the barn, leaving Kiff laughing behind her.

"Whoa," Kiff said. "Did you see her face, Odie? She was really mad!"

His friend, Odie Pedersen, popped up from behind Dinah, his horse. The three of them met every day to feed and groom their horses in Odie's old cedar barn on the shore of Big Pickle Lake. Odie shook his head. "I wish you'd stop bugging Josie about that old fort."

"Old Moonbrain?" Kiff looked surprised. "Bugging her just comes naturally." He lifted down a forkful of hay for his grey horse, Smoke, and laughed again. "Anyway, I'll get her to tell me how to find Fort James. We still have a week before school starts to get there."

"Well, I wish you'd give up the whole idea." Odie smoothed the brush down Dinah's side. "Do me a favour and don't mention that old fort when she comes back."

But at that moment, the roar of an outboard motor told them that Josie was not coming back, not even to finish feeding her horse, Skydive. From the barn door, the two boys could see her fast boat, the *Green Hornet*, buzzing across the blue water of the lake.

Odie sighed. "I wish you wouldn't tease Josie so much."

"But we've been teasing Josie for centuries!" Kiff peered at his friend in astonishment. "Why stop now?"

"Well, I ... she doesn't deserve it, sometimes." Odie glanced at Kiff. "I think she's okay ... sometimes."

"You *like* her?" This was such an impossible thought that Kiff sat down with a plop on a heap of straw. "Odie, you can't like Josie Moon. We've been sworn enemies since we were six. *She's* the enemy."

Odie wasn't saying anything. His cheeks were flaming, his ears were red, and Kiff could see pink scalp between his spikes of blond hair.

"I should have seen this coming," Kiff shouted. He shot to his feet. "You've been sticking up for Josie all summer. Now I know why. You like her!"

Kiff slammed the door of Smoke's stall and tore out of the barn. He and Odie had always been a team. The two of them against old know-it-all Moon with her fast green boat and her stuck-up way of talking.

He should have seen it coming. Well, if Odie *had* joined the enemy he would be sorry! He could expect no mercy. Nobody was easier to tease than Odie. You could make him blush by calling out his name in a crowd. Just wait, Odie, Kiff thought. You will be sorry you were ever nice to Josie Moon!

Kiff's head was full of schemes as he raced towards the town of Big Pickle Lake. It was a perfect time to go exploring in the woods. Back in the bush the bugs would be almost gone, the blueberries still ripe and juicy. Ever since Kiff had heard they were digging in the ruins of an old fort near Big Pickle Lake, he had been itching to have a look at it.

But he'd have to find it first, and Josie was the key. Her father's Cree ancestors had traded furs at Fort James. Josie knew where it was. And somehow, she was going to lead him there.

Kiff slowed down to a walk, heading for the town dock. He would wait there for his dad to pick him up in their boat, *The Big Queen*. Kiff lived at a fishing camp on Big Pickle Island. At this time of year, most of the fishermen were gone. The town dock was deserted.

But suddenly, Kiff heard something that made his ears pop. Someone was calling for help! He darted forward towards the dock.

2

The Red Drool

As he raced toward the town dock, Kiff tried to sort out what was happening. At the end of the long cedar dock he saw a girl, crouching over something large and reddish brown.

"Help me, he's dying!" the girl screamed when she saw Kiff pounding down the boards towards them.

"What's wrong?" Kiff shouted. Now he could see the big mass of red hair was a dog, thrashing and howling and making terrible sounds in his throat.

"He's choking," the girl cried. "Somehow he got his collar stuck. I don't know what happened, he was just lying down and when he went to get up ... "

"Hold him still," Kiff ordered. "Sit on him, if you have to."

"Drool, good boy, lie still." The girl threw herself across the dog's struggling body.

Kiff kept his hands away from the dog's huge teeth and powerful jaws. He thrust his hands into the thick red hair. His fingers touched hot strangling links of steel biting into the dog's neck.

The dog was wearing a choke collar! Somehow the ring at the end of the collar was twisted down between the boards of the dock. The more he struggled the more the collar choked off his air! Kiff got a finger between the cruel steel and the dog's windpipe and felt the dog gulp a huge lungful of air.

The dog thrashed wildly, but couldn't lift his head.

"Easy fellow," Kiff said. He shifted his position to wiggle his pocket knife out of his pocket and handed it to the girl. "Open the knife for me — try to find the saw blade. I have to keep my finger in his collar to give him air."

The girl yanked at the blades. She finally snapped open the small saw and handed it back to Kiff.

With one hand, Kiff stabbed and dug at the soft old wood between the boards. It was hard to see with the dog's hair in the way, but if he could just make the crack a little wider ...

"What are you doing?" the girl cried. "Don't hurt him!"

"I'm trying to get this ring loose," Kiff grunted. "Why have you got a choke collar on him?

They're deadly." At that instant the chain popped free.

In a flash the dog was on his feet, hurling the girl to one side as he tore down the dock.

"Stop, Drool! Come back!" the girl shouted, and raced off after him.

Kiff sat back, stunned. Quick recovery, he thought. He had never seen a dog run so fast.

But in another flash the flying red fury was back, thundering down the dock. He swirled around Kiff with a quick lick on the ear that nearly knocked him into the lake. Kiff made a grab but the dog was off again, running circles around the sandy parking lot.

The girl staggered up waving the empty leash. "*Now* do you see why we have a choke collar on him?" she panted. "He's too fast ... too strong. I'm so afraid he'll get hit by a car!"

"Not too many cars around," Kiff pointed to the empty parking lot. "Anyway, in Big Pickle Lake cars usually look out for dogs."

"That's a relief." The girl plopped down beside Kiff. "I just hope he comes back. He hasn't had much chance to run free like this ... "

"Throw a stick for him," Kiff suggested. "When he brings it back, you can get his leash on."

"It might work." The girl looked doubtful. "He loves sticks." She ran down the dock and picked up a piece of driftwood from the shore. "Here, Drool, stick!" she shouted, throwing it towards him. Drool barked joyfully and caught the stick in the air.

"Bring it here, Drool," she called, but Drool had no idea of giving up his precious stick. He pranced down the dock towards Kiff again, growling happily with the driftwood in his mouth, daring him to try to take it away.

Kiff grabbed the driftwood and held on while the girl dashed up and managed to clip on the leash. Then all three collapsed, Drool chewing on his stick, Kiff and the girl staring at each other.

Her hair was almost exactly the same colour as the dog's, Kiff realized, and her eyes were reddish brown too. She was taller than he was, and thinner. Her clothes and sandals looked city-ish, but now that the colour had come back to her face her skin was brown, as though she'd spent the summer outside.

"I'm Dee," she said. "Thank you for saving Drool's life."

"Drool is his name?" Kiff said. At the sound of his name, the dog was on his feet like a flash, licking their faces. He had been running hard and drooling. Kiff's shirt was soon covered in dog slobber. "Never mind," Kiff laughed. "I think I know how he got it!"

"You should see it at home," Dee sighed. "After he takes a drink he leaves a trail of dog slobber from one end of the kitchen to the other."

"Nice-looking dog, though," Kiff mumbled. Drool was now whipping them both in the face with his big red plume of a tail. Drool had to be the stupidest dog Kiff had ever seen. Imagine a dog who wouldn't play fetch!

"I don't know how he got that chain caught in between the boards like that," Kiff said. "What a freak accident!"

"Not really," Dee said, "if you knew Drool."

"You mean he's sort of accident prone?" Kiff asked.

"More like trouble prone," Dee sighed. "I guess because he's so big and bouncy. He's always getting into stuff."

Kiff suddenly felt more sympathetic towards Drool. People often said the same thing about him.

"What's your name?" Dee asked.

"Kiff Kokatow."

Dee didn't laugh or even say his name was funny. She just nodded. "Do you live here?"

"Yes. Well, no. I live on that island over there," Kiff pointed towards Big Pickle Island. "We have a fishing camp."

"Cool," Dee sighed, looking longingly at the green island in the blue lake. "I wish I could get out in the woods. We're staying at the hotel. My parents dig up things for the museum. They're visiting some friends who are digging up an old fort. My job is looking after Drool, but there's nowhere in town where he can run."

Kiff's brain went into overdrive. "Did you say your parents are digging up Fort James?"

"They're helping," Dee agreed. "They're archaeologists."

"Can I come and visit you at the hotel tomorrow?" Kiff asked quickly. He could see their boat, the *Queen,* coming towards the dock. But he wanted to make sure he would see this girl again.

"Sure!" She looked pleased. "But I'll only be there till ten-thirty. Then we're going out on the dig."

"That will be great. I have to go now," Kiff said, looking over his shoulder. "I'll see you tomorrow." The *Queen* was almost at the dock and the noise of her twin engines was drowning them out.

Dee managed a wave as Kiff jumped aboard. When he looked back, he could see her being dragged down the dock on the end of Drool's leash.

3

The Big Pickle Lake Hotel

The next day Kiff was at Odie's barn early, telling him all about Dee. "So will you come up to the hotel with me?" he asked Odie.

Odie was grooming Dinah. "Do you think Dee knows how to get to the fort?" he asked.

"Of course," Kiff said. "Her parents are ar-chi..archi..whatevers. They work at Fort James. Maybe you and I and Dee could get there by canoe. I don't know about taking that dog though ... "

"Now you're talking about going on a canoe trip with this girl," Odie shook his head. "I don't believe I'm hearing this from Kokatow, the Josie hater. What's so special about this girl?"

"Well, she's not like *Josie Moon*," Kiff said. "Nothing like her. You'll see. C'mon. They're leaving the hotel at ten-thirty."

A fully loaded Jeep was parked in front of the Big Pickle Lake Hotel. The hotel was an old wood building, painted white with green

trim. The rooms above the bar were hardly ever used. It was probably the only place in town that would take a dog like Drool, Kiff thought.

Inside it was dark and smelled like beer. A few tough-looking guys were sitting around a small round table in the bar. There was nobody at the desk. "How are we going to find this girl?" Odie asked.

All at once there was an explosion of noise from upstairs. Doors banged, voices were raised, and something came hurtling down the stairs.

"Watch out!" Kiff shouted. In another second Drool threw himself at Kiff, a hurricane of red fur. He leaped on his chest to lick his face, twisted around his legs, whined and yelped and slobbered. Kiff laughed. "Down! Enough! I'm glad to see you too."

Then two pairs of feet came clattering down the dark staircase. Kiff looked up from the blur of dog. "Hi, Dee," he said, smiling. In the next instant, the smile was swept away. "JOSIE MOON!" he cried. "What in the thundering dust are you doing here?"

The four of them stood staring at each other in the small front hall of the hotel.

"My parents dropped me off on the way to work," Josie said. Her mom and dad were wild-life experts, working for the government. Every morning they travelled from Little Pickle Island, where Josie lived, to their jobs on the mainland.

"Her mom went to university with my mom," Dee smiled at Kiff. "It's so great. Now I know two people here."

"One person and one stuck up know-it-all," Kiff muttered under his breath.

"I told Josie how you saved Drool's life," Dee said. Drool was still whirling and thumping around, jumping on one person after another.

"It's nice to know you can be intelligent when you want to, Kiff," Josie patted the dog's silky red head. "And this is Odie Pedersen, my friend, who has the farm where we keep our horses."

Odie was already blushing. He turned away and pretended to be staring at a poster for a horse auction tacked up in the hotel hallway.

"I thought it would be great if Dee comes out to the farm with us. We need a fourth person to ride Efstur. That's the valuable Icelandic Horse I was telling you about," Josie explained to Dee. "Our friend left him with us over the winter and we want to ride him every day if we can. What do you think, Odie?"

"Sure," Odie shrugged, turning back.

"Great, just great," Kiff muttered to himself. Josie Moon, horning in again! Wouldn't you know, just wouldn't you know that she would find out about Dee and get here before him. He wanted to invite Dee to Odie's farm, but Josie had stolen the idea. It was so typical, so Josie Moonish!

Dee looked hurt. "What's the matter Kiff? Don't you want me to come?"

"No, I mean sure ... we need another rider because we have four horses instead of three now and ... "

"Don't mind him, "Josie said. "He has this big thing about hating girls. Just ignore him."

Just then, Drool made a break for it. He dashed into the bar, ran around the small round tables, and jumped up on one of the drinkers. The man's arm jerked back and beer splashed down his plaid shirt.

"Get him out of here!" the man growled.

"I'm sorry," Dee apologized. "Sit, Drool." It took all four of them to make him sit while Dee snapped the leash on his collar.

"I suppose he's a *valuable* dog, just like your horses," one of the other men sneered. "Where's he from — Upper Slobovia?"

"He's a champion Irish setter ..." Dee started to say, but Kiff grabbed her arm and dragged her and Drool away.

"Better not say too much to Stan and Morley," he told her when they were all outside in the sunshine again.

Dee looked angry. "We call them *the louts*," she said. "My dad said they looked harmless enough. They're always in there, drinking beer."

"When they're not drinking beer, Stan and Morley are looking for something to steal so they can buy more beer," Kiff told her.

"Oh." Dee looked worried. "I'll tell my parents. Maybe they shouldn't leave the truck here," Dee pointed to the loaded Jeep. "It's full of equipment and valuable artifacts from the fort. We're taking it all back to Toronto."

"Maybe you should stay at our fishing camp," Kiff said quickly. "Your stuff would be safe there."

Josie jumped in. "Don't be silly Kiff. How could they get the truck over to Camp Kokatow? Anyway, she's going to stay with me this week. We're going on a canoe trip and you're not invited ... Come on, Dee, I'll race you up the street." They dashed off, laughing, with Drool leaping around their flying feet.

"See? *See?*" Kiff shouted. "That girl ruins everything."

"But did you really want a *girl* at Camp Koka-tow?" Odie said. "That's a first. Usually you'd rather have a week of rain than girls at the camp."

"But this was part of my plan," Kiff explained. "If Dee and her parents were at the camp, I could get them talking about old forts, where to find them ... "

"Not that again," Odie groaned.

"Yes, *that* again. Instead of having Dee at the camp, she's going to be at Josie's all week. I'll never get to talk to her. That girl ... " Kiff looked after Josie and shook his fist. "Sometimes I really hate that girl!"

4

Moonster Knows Best

"Which horse do you want to ride?" Josie was asking Dee as Kiff and Odie came panting into the barn.

Dee stood entranced in front of Efstur's stall. She ruffled the frosty gold forelock that fell over his eyes. "He's so adorable!" she cried. "I've never seen a horse like this!"

"And you probably never will again," Kiff came up and held Efstur's bridle while she stroked the little horse's velvety nose. "Efstur means 'the best' in Icelandic. And he is the best. He's a dream to ride."

"He can be a bit frisky," Josie warned, "if you're not used to him. Smoke and Dinah are gentler."

"Who asked you?" Kiff snapped. "I'm sure she can handle Ef." He glared at Josie. She glared back, her dark eyes blazing in the shadowy barn.

"Maybe I'd better try an easier horse," Dee said. "I haven't ridden much."

"Efstur's *fine*," Kiff said through gritted teeth. "Old Moon just likes to butt in."

"Who's butting in?" Josie said angrily. "Dee and I were fine until you came along!" By now she and Kiff were standing hands on hips, furious nose to furious nose.

Odie led his brown mare, Dinah, between Josie and Kiff, forcing them apart. "Are we going to ride today, or just stand in the barn and listen to you two fight?" he asked.

He grinned at Dee, who looked shocked and worried. "Don't mind them," he sighed. "They do this all the time. It's a good thing my grandfather doesn't allow fighting in the barn or they'd be hurling horse buns at each other."

"Your grandfather?" Dee asked.

"It's his barn," Odie explained. "This is his farm, but he lets us keep our horses here. *If* we follow the rules," he added loudly.

"All right, all right!" Kiff threw up his hands. "Ride Smoke. See if I care. The Moonster knows best!" He pulled a battered carrot out of his back pocket and offered it to Smoke, who poked her head out of the stall next to Efstur. She was a tall mare, the colour of pale grey smoke. She lipped the carrot gently from Kiff's hand and stood quietly munching.

"It's such a great place," Dee looked around the sunlit barn. "I wish I could come back here next summer."

"Why can't you?" Kiff was leading Smoke out of the stall for her.

"Well, the money for the dig is all used up," Dee explained. "They haven't found anything really important at Fort James this summer, so they probably won't get any more money to keep going."

"What would be really important?" Kiff asked, his eyes lighting up. He took the horse brush from the shelf and started grooming Smoke. He always did this before the afternoon ride.

"I don't really know," Dee shrugged. "Something with a date on it, I guess."

Josie was grooming Skydive on the other side of the barn. She looked over at Kiff and tossed her head. "What do you care, Kokatow? Yesterday you said that an old fort wasn't worth anything." She laughed. "Isn't that what you said?"

"Well, I didn't mean ... I don't think ... " Kiff could see Dee was looking puzzled and a bit hurt. "I mean, it would be if they found something really *important.*"

How could Kiff explain to Dee that he was only trying to bug Josie when he said that? Old Moonface again. She was always telling on him, twisting his words, getting him in trouble.

"I bet I could find something exciting," he said. "I'm good at finding stuff."

"You?" Josie laughed again. "Finding yourself in a fix, that's what you do best!"

"Hey, what about that fishing spot I found, where we caught the prizewinning pike? What about the gold I found in the cave? What about these horses?" Kiff waved around the barn. "I could find anything at that old fort!"

"I found the horses!" Josie cried. "And you will never get near the fort, if I have anything to do with it. You'll just mess it up, and tell all the tourists at Camp Kokatow where it is, and treat it like some kind of a joke!"

Dee was gazing from one to the other in amazement. "Do they really fight like this all the time?" she asked.

"*All* the time," Odie sighed. "Come on you guys, this is stupid. Let's get out there and ride."

A few minutes later they led the groomed and saddled horses out of the barn. Efstur's blonde mane and glowing chestnut body were even more dramatic in the sunlight. He tossed his mane in joy at being outdoors. In his native Iceland, Efstur would have lived outside winter and summer.

Kiff was still fuming. He and Odie rode behind the two girls, on the dirt road that ran along the shore of Big Pickle Lake. "I know they're hatching something," Kiff mumbled.

"What are you grumbling about now?" Odie asked.

"I'm telling you they've got a scheme — a plan to sneak off to Fort James without us. You know that canoe trip Josie was talking about? I'll bet that's where they're going."

"So?" Odie grinned. "Think they'll ask us along?"

"Not likely!" Kiff shook his head. "But if those girls think they're going to sneak off in a canoe and visit Fort James without us, they're wrong!"

5

All Dogs Can Swim!

The green canoe was just a dot in the distance as it came around the end of Big Pickle Island and headed into the open lake.

"There they go," Kiff said, shaking his head in disgust. "Without us."

It was the next day. Kiff and Odie had been waiting at the farm for Josie and Dee for more than an hour with horses saddled.

"I can't believe they took Drool in the canoe with them," Odie said. "I haven't seen that dumb dog sit still for more than two seconds. He'll tip them over!"

"He'll slow them down," Kiff said. "And that will give us time to ride to the end of the lake and cut them off at the portage. Let's go." He swung his leg over Efstur's sturdy back and settled into the saddle.

Efstur was a champion Icelandic horse, but he was no pampered show pony. He was at home in the Canadian north. His strong feet could fly over the rough rocky ground with amazing ease, and he could stay outside in the coldest weather.

Odie was riding Smoke. The big grey mare and the little chestnut Icelander made an odd couple as they rode away from the farm on the lakeshore.

Their route took them through the town of Big Pickle Lake. They stayed off the town's one paved street, following side streets. On one of the streets a rusty yellow pickup was parked by the side of the road.

"Hey! Nice horses." The truck horn blared, making Smoke dance with fear. "Get the joke? *Hay* is for horses!"

"Way to go, horsey, let's get spooked," called a second voice from the cab of the truck.

"It's those dumb guys from the hotel," Odie cursed. "Easy, Smoke."

"C'mon, let's get out of here," Kiff urged Ef into a gallop, heading for the end of the street, where it turned into an old mining road that led south along the lake.

Behind them, the two men leaned out the windows of the cab. "It looks like this is our chance," the one called Morley said. "How much did the guy at the auction say one of them Icelandic horses might be worth?"

Stan reached for the rolled-up auction poster he had stuffed behind the seat. On it he had scribbled a number. "About $10,000," he said.

Morley's eyes and mouth were watering. "Then what are we waiting for?" he asked. "Let's *borrow* Bruce's horse van and go after them."

* * *

Out on the lake, Josie struggled to keep the canoe steady. "Drool, sit still," she ordered. The big red dog, perched in the middle of the canoe, looked miserable.

"I'm so glad I met you," Dee turned over her shoulder to grin at Josie. "My parents left my brothers and sisters with my aunt, but they couldn't leave Drool, so I had to come to look after him. It was pretty boring until Kiff showed up. What's he like?"

"Totally hopeless," Josie said. But she wasn't going to think about Kiff today. "It's great for me to have someone to go canoeing with," she called to Dee.

"How about Odie?" Dee asked. "He seems pretty nice."

"Odie's not bad if you can get him away from Kiff," Josie said. "But that's the problem. He and Kiff have been getting into trouble so long, it's a habit, and Odie just goes along … Drool! Sit down!"

Drool was trying to make himself comfortable. It was hard for a big dog in a small space. It took a lot of walking in circles before you could flop just right, and he didn't like the way the canoe kept moving around.

"SIT!" Dee commanded. Drool finally found a spot and collapsed. Unfortunately he collapsed on one side of the canoe, and the two girls felt the whole canoe dip wildly.

"I hope we don't tip," Dee said nervously. "I don't think Drool can swim."

"All dogs can swim!" Josie said, but looking at Drool she suddenly wondered if that were true. If they dumped, they would have a long swim from the middle of the lake.

"Do you think the guys minded very much that we're going to the fort without them?" As Dee swung around to ask, her red hair flipped over her shoulder.

"Listen, Dee," Josie panted. "They're not *the guys*. They're just stupid boys. Kiff and Odie. Bird brains. Drool has more sense than both of them put together."

Drool lunged at Josie when he heard his name. He hated the way the wind was shoving the canoe over and slapping water against the side. A wave had washed over his long nose the last time he poked it over the edge.

"Tell him to sit still, for heaven's sake," Josie dug hard with her paddle, trying to keep the canoe level. She was losing the battle against the wind and Drool wasn't helping.

"Lie down, you big lug," Dee ordered, but Drool, as usual, paid no attention. Instead he tried to walk up the canoe to her, but got stuck behind one of the seats.

"If he tries to climb over that we're sunk!" Josie thought. The wind was blowing them towards the east shore of the lake and away from the portage and the river that led to the old fort. With a good paddler — and no big red dog — she could have danced with the wind, making short tacks back and forth up the lake. With Dee thinking about *the guys* and Drool, they were as helpless as floating driftwood!

Sure enough, half an hour later they were bashing against the rocks on the east shore. The portage was two kilometres away and it might as well have been on the moon. The wind was howling down at them, and Drool howled back.

"Arooo," he mourned, wanting to be anywhere but stuck in a tippy canoe in this storm ...

"Now what do we do?" Dee asked.

Josie was resting her weary arm muscles. Her paddle lay across her knees. "We've got three choices," she sighed. "One, sit here until the wind dies down. Two, try to paddle along the shore into the wind, which will take all day. Three ... " but she never got to three. Drool had had enough of canoeing.

"Aroo-oo-oo," he howled, drowning her out.

"Drool votes for the third choice, " Josie laughed. " ... which is, get out and walk along the shore, pulling the canoe. It's light, it will float over most of the rocks and sunken logs without us in it. We can tow it to the portage."

"Good," Dee sounded relieved. "But where can we land?" she asked, looking at the thick tangle of sunken logs and slippery rocks between the canoe and the shore.

"Good question," Josie said. "Paddle hard on your left side, and we'll see how close we can get. LIE DOWN!" she yelled at Drool, who was trying to get out the front of the boat by climbing over Dee.

"Wait, Drool," she warned him, but he scrambled over the seat, dived past Dee, shot off the bow of the canoe, and landed with a loud splash in the water.

"Oh, no," Dee shouted. "I'm telling you, he can't swim!"

6

Where Are They?

Meanwhile, Kiff and Odie had ridden to the portage at the south end of the lake.

"Where are they?" Kiff slid off Efstur's back and threw the reins over the little horse's shoulder.

"Not here yet," Odie was already examining the mud by the shore. "I don't see any marks from the canoe or dog tracks ... Man, it looks rough out there."

The waves were scudding into the bay, bits of white foam forming on their tops. The wind whipped the poplars along the shore, filling the air with golden leaves.

"Josie will be having a tough time paddling against that wind," Kiff agreed. "Good, I'm glad we got here first. It allows me to put my plan into action."

"What plan?" Odie asked. "You said we were coming here to help the girls over the portage. That's why I agreed to come." He stood glaring at Kiff, his shoulders thrown back, his hair bristling.

"Well, you see, we'll leave the horses here and ... " Kiff started to say, then stopped. "I'm not sure I can trust you any more, Odie," he said.

They stared at each other in silence. "Don't tell me," Odie finally said. "It's probably some dumb dangerous plan that gets us all in trouble ... So, are we going to wait here and help the girls, or ride back to town — which is it?"

"I hate the way you say *the girls* as if they were special," Kiff snorted. "I just wanted to surprise them a little."

"But they're going to know we're here when they see the horses," Odie pointed out. "I vote we climb the hill and see where they are." He looped Smoke's reins around a tree. "They might be in trouble in that wind."

"I don't believe this ... " Kiff muttered, but he was already tying Efstur nearby. In the back of his mind he had a picture of the canoe battling the waves. He wished Odie wouldn't keep talking about trouble. Josie could stand up to a hurricane, but he wasn't sure about Dee. And as for that dog ... !

* * *

Frantically, Drool's front paws scrabbled at the water.

"We've got to help him," Dee's brown eyes were wide with alarm. "He's sinking!"

"He won't sink ... " Josie started to say, then realized Dee was right. The black water closed over Drool's head. He came up, clawed the air, and sank again.

"Here," Josie thrust the canoe rope into Dee's hand. "I'll get him." She slipped into the neck-deep water, grabbed handfuls of red fur, and shoved the struggling dog towards the shore.

Dee reached out to grab his collar. "I've got you, Droo, it's okay, come on boy ... " Drool dragged himself up on a rock and was sick. He had swallowed a lot of water.

"Who ever heard of a dog that couldn't dog-paddle," Josie said in disgust, hauling herself onto the rocks. She was soaked through and freezing. This dog was just a bundle of trouble! "Come on. You take Drool away from the water, and I'll drag the canoe ... Dee! Where's the canoe?"

A look of horror swept over Dee's face. Josie whipped her head around and saw her green canoe quickly disappearing down the lake, as light as a leaf, as swift as a bird.

"You let go!" Josie groaned. "You let go of the rope."

"I forgot ... I was trying to reach for him. Oh, Josie, I'm sorry!" Dee looked stricken. "Can we get it back ... somehow?"

"Nope," Josie sighed. "It's just plain amazing how fast and how far a canoe can go when you drop that rope. It's okay, Dee. We've all done it."

"Even Kiff?" Dee asked.

"Especially Kiff," Josie shook her head. "You've got to get rid of this idea that he's some kind of hero. He once sank a whole fleet of fishing boats by forgetting to put the drain plugs back in them." Josie sighed. "Believe me, if Kokatow were along on this trip, we'd be in even worse trouble than we are now!"

* * *

Kiff and Odie were panting when they reached the top of the bluff overlooking the lake. From here they could see nothing but water and trees. The cool air had started to turn the birch and poplar leaves so that patches of gold showed up against the dark evergreens.

Up here the wind was strong, and the smell of spruce sap swirled in the air. Odie swept the shoreline with binoculars. "Don't see them," he said.

"I see something! Give me those!" Kiff snatched the glasses and stared down the lake. "There's a green canoe ... drifting ... way down by Sandy Point ... look!" He thrust the binoculars back at Odie.

Odie found the green dot, bobbing swiftly away from them. "It's Josie's canoe," he said. "But there's nobody in it."

"So where are they?" Kiff looked worried. "If they capsized in the middle of the lake, the canoe would be upside down, wouldn't it?"

"Unless it flipped really fast and tossed them out ... " Odie agreed. He was thinking of the dog in the canoe.

"We'd better get down there," Kiff pointed to the shore. "They must be in some kind of trouble." He started to run back the way they had come.

"So you care about her after all," Odie panted.

"Care about who? *Moonbrain?*" Kiff yelled over his shoulder. "You've got to be kidding! I was thinking about Drool. Dee says he can't swim."

7

Horsenappers!

Josie and Dee could move much faster without dragging the canoe along the shore.

"The portage is right over there," Josie pointed to a clearing at the shoreline. "A road leads to it," she explained, squishing along in her wet running shoes. "Maybe we can hitch a ride back to town."

"There's a truck there now," Dee pointed to the clearing. The nose of a rusty yellow pickup could be glimpsed through the trees.

"Hold on," Josie gripped Dee's arm. "I know that truck."

As they moved closer they heard a high, frightened whinny and angry shouts. The sounds were coming from behind the truck.

"Come on," Josie urged. They made a circle through the trees around the edge of the clearing until they could see what was happening.

"The boys' horses," Josie whispered. She could see flashes of grey and chestnut as the horses milled around.

"Isn't that ... ?"

"Stan and Morley," Josie nodded. The two men from the hotel were trying to shove Efstur into a battered grey horse van hitched to the truck. He gave an angry whinny and lashed out with his hind feet.

Josie dashed forward. "What are you doing!" she shouted. "Those are our horses!"

The man named Morley was still struggling to get Efstur into the van. "I don't think so," he shouted back over his shoulder. "We just found them here in the woods, left on their own."

"Anyway," the man named Stan added, "it was two boys we saw riding these horses. Not you." He had Smoke by the bridle. "We thought we'd just give them a lift back to town."

"You're lying!" Josie was furious. "You're stealing those horses, and you know it!" She ran up to Morley and tried to pull Efstur away from him.

"Butt out of what's not your business," he growled and elbowed Josie away. "If people leave horses just standing around in the bush, they can't care very much about them. C'mon, little fellow, let's get aboard ... " He gave Efstur a hard smack on his rump, and Efstur at last disappeared into the rusty old van.

"Now for the big grey one," Morley said. "Bring her up here, Stan."

"No," Josie bellowed. "You're not taking her!" She flew to Smoke's side. If she could get on her back, she could ride her out of there. She grabbed Smoke round the neck and tried to get her foot in the stirrup.

But Drool, who had been dancing around, enjoying the commotion, wanted to get in the game. He grabbed the leg of Josie's jeans between his big teeth and tugged. That gave Morley the time he needed to knock Josie away and get on the other side of Smoke.

"NOT ME! BITE THEM, DROOL," Josie cried. "ATTACK!"

"Looks like the dog's on our side." Morley laughed. "Thanks Big Red!" Between them they loaded Smoke into the van and slammed shut the metal doors.

"What's the matter with that dog!" Josie said furiously. Morley heaved his big meaty body behind the wheel and Stan, who was about half his size, clambered into the passenger side. The truck swung in a circle, bumping the horse van over the rough ground.

"He'd never attack," Dee said, sadly, patting Drool's big head. "He thinks life's a big party." Drool flopped over on the mossy ground to get his underside rubbed. "What are we going to do?"

"I wish we had that canoe!" Josie's voice was low and desperate. From inside the moving horse van they could hear Efstur's frightened neighing.

"They'll be miles away before we get help," Josie groaned. "If they hurt those horses ... " She looked after the disappearing van and shook her fist.

"The licence number!" Dee said. "Remember 464 CYD." She let go of Drool, and he bounced to his feet, shaking out a shower of moss and pine needles.

"I don't understand," Dee said, looking around the clearing. "How did the horses get away out here?"

"I smell the work of Kiff Kokatow," Josie said. "I'll bet he and Odie are around here somewhere ... Kiff, Odie ... " she shouted. "Come on, Dee, help me yell!"

Halfway down the hill, Odie and Kiff heard the distant echo of their names, and Drool, howling.

"That's Josie," Kiff said. "I'd know her moose call anywhere!" He swung around a birch tree to slow his downward hurtle. "They must be okay. I hear two voices *and* that dog."

Odie's face was red with running, and now relief. "It sounds like they're at the portage," he exclaimed. "How did they get there without the canoe?"

Kiff grinned at him. "It probably wasn't Josie's canoe we saw drifting. We were all worried for nothing." His face clouded. "But how do they know we're here?"

Odie looked disgusted. "Are you still playing dumb games? Of course they know we're here. They see the horses! Come on, Kiff. Admit you're a little bit glad they're all right."

Kiff grinned. "Maybe," he laughed. "But don't ever tell Josie Moon."

A few minutes later, Drool came crashing through the brush. He dashed up to them, whipping their legs with his tail and dancing circles around them.

"Drool, you old fool, what are you doing here?"

"Look, he's wet, but all in one piece ... "

As they came into the clearing, Josie ran to meet them. Her face looked like a thunder cloud. Her dark brown eyes shot lightning. "Kiff Kokatow, where have you been?"

Kiff laughed. "Easy to see where you've been — in the lake with all your clothes on," he said. "And what do you care where we've been?" He threw Odie a look that said this is what you get for caring about Josie Moon!

"The *horses*, Kokatow. You left them here."

"So?"

"So, Eftsur and Smoke are in the back of a horse van ... and you just *left* them here ... to be stolen!" Josie was so angry she was almost speechless.

"What van?" Kiff and Odie raced over to the trees where they had tied the horses. The deep tire tracks in the moss, straw thrown out of the back of the van in the struggle, a tangle of hoof prints in the soft ground. It was all there to tell the story. Kiff looked at Josie with a shocked face. "Who took them?"

"Stan and Morley," Josie said. "I tried to stop them. How could you do it Kiff? Ride the horses out here, and then just wander off and leave them?" Her brown eyes were blazing.

"You see what you get?" Kiff shouted at Odie. "You see what you get for worrying about *girls*? See what you get for climbing hills trying to save them?"

"Is that what you were doing?" Dee asked. "Josie thought you were trying to play a trick on us and keep us from getting to the fort."

"Trick schmick! Get the canoe. We have to get back to town." Kiff raced for the shore where the canoe should be. He stared wildly around. "Where is it?

"There is no canoe," Josie called. "We lost it … "

"I let go of the rope when Josie was trying to save Drool," Dee ran after him to explain. Drool seemed to know something terrible had happened, and that it was somehow his fault.

He whined miserably and thrust his wet nose into Kiff's hand.

"You are the stupidest dog I have ever met," Kiff said. "It's a good thing I had my little surprise all planned."

8

Kiff's Surprise

The other three gaped at him. "What surprise?" Josie said, suspiciously.

"We've all been incredibly dumb," Kiff said. "You know better than to try to paddle a canoe with a big red dog in it! I'm sure Dee knows better than to let a canoe go drifting away in a high wind. And I know better than to leave the horses and go tearing off trying to rescue somebody who has never needed rescuing in her life!" He glared at Josie. "But that doesn't matter now. We have to get Smoke and Efstur back. So just help me and no lectures!"

He took off at a run down the portage trail, Drool at his heels. There had been too much standing around talking to suit him. "Arooo!" he howled, as if to say "Let's go!"

After a quick look at each other, Josie, Dee, and Odie followed. The trail snaked through the trees. It had been beaten down by thousands of pairs of feet. Native people had used the portage for countless years. Then the fur traders had portaged canoes and heavy packs from Big Pickle Lake to Rankin River. Somewhere down that river was the ruins of Fort James, the fur trading post.

The portage was half a kilometre long. When they were close enough to hear the river bubbling along, Kiff suddenly detoured into a patch of young pines. They could hear him and Drool crashing around, and then the hollow *thump, thump* of Drool's powerful tail hitting something.

It was Josie who recognized the sound first. "He's got another canoe stashed in those trees!" she said. "That's his surprise. You were going to follow us," she blazed at Kiff.

Kiff was dragging the red canoe out of the brush. "I hid it just in case you tried to sneak away without us," Kiff flashed back. "And I was right!"

"So you were just going to leave the horses in the clearing," Josie said.

"Who knew the louts were going to come along?" Kiff shrugged.

"They must have followed us from town," Odie groaned.

"Who cares!" Kiff bellowed. "Every second, Smoke and Ef are getting farther away." Kiff hoisted one end of the small canoe on his shoulders and Odie took the other.

They hurried back over the portage, launching the canoe back into the windswept lake.

Getting Drool back in a canoe, however, was a different story. The big red dog refused. He bounced in a circle and growled when they tried to get him aboard.

"Now what?" Kiff was exasperated. "Maybe we should leave him here."

"No!" Dee protested. "Or if you have to leave him, leave me too."

Kiff looked at her, standing with one hand in Drool's fur, the other holding back her own long red hair. He shook his head. "We're all going," he sighed. "You and I can hold Drool down in the middle of the canoe. Josie and Odie will paddle."

Josie couldn't believe it. She knew she was a better paddler than Kiff, but she had not expected him to admit it. He would hate sitting in the bottom of a boat, holding down a dog.

They finally got Drool in the canoe by throwing a stick into the bottom. He hated water, but he'd go anywhere to chase a stick! Dee and Kiff sat facing each other, with the dog between them. Kiff held his collar, while Dee kept his rear end on the bottom of the boat. Drool wiggled and squirmed and complained. Josie paddled in the bow and Odie in the stern. Once they were afloat, they were so heavy that the water lapped just below the gunnels.

"Whatever you do," Odie warned, "don't let him make a sudden move!"

Kiff looked down at Drool's long, sorrowful face. The dog's wrinkled brow went up and down as he tried to understand why he was being held down. "Don't worry," Kiff soothed. "You're going to lie still, and we're going to be fine."

Drool licked his shoe.

Kiff grinned at Dee. "Paddle like fury," he called back to Odie. "We've got the dog situation under control."

The wind was behind them now. It blew them back down Big Pickle Lake as if the heavily loaded canoe were as light as a feather. The white caps on the lake were higher, and the wind blew the foam off the tops. Josie, paddling hard in the front, knew that it was unsafe to be out on the open water with this much wind. She knew Odie would know it too.

They were keeping their nose pointing straight with the wind. If a wave hit them broadside, they'd be over in a flash. If only Kiff and Dee could keep Drool still until they got safely to shore!

Just then she heard a cry from Dee, who was sitting behind her, facing the wind. Her words floated up to Josie.

"That cloud! Look!"

She and Kiff turned to look, careful not to move their bodies suddenly. Kiff kept a good grip on Drool's collar. A huge black cloud was hurrying down the lake behind them. Streamers of rain blocked out the sky.

"It's a squall, Odie," Kiff yelled. "Going to hit any minute. Drive for shore!"

Odie threw a quick glance over his shoulder and dug his paddle in hard. The canoe, now at an angle to the waves, leaped even faster forward, aimed like an arrow at the shore.

All three of the Big Pickle Lake kids knew no canoe could survive one of the quick violent storms that blew up when the weather changed like this.

It got suddenly dark as night as the squall prepared to pounce. Thunder rumbled behind them.

"Oh no!" Dee cried above the wind. "Drool is terrified of thunder. He'll go crazy. At home he hides in the bathtub!"

Kiff tore off his shirt. In a few seconds he was going to be so wet it wouldn't matter anyway. He covered Drool's head with the cloth, and then leaned his body over the shivering animal. "It's okay, buddy," he told Drool. "Just a little storm." Lie still, whatever you do, he thought. We'll never survive if we're swamped in this wind.

Another second and the lightning struck, flashing all around them. The thunder crashed, right over their heads.

Odie and Josie fought the wind, trying to hold the canoe steady in its wild gusts and reach the shore.

9

The Sound of Kicking

"Go, go, go!" Kiff shouted over the shrieking wind. "We're almost there!"

As the blast of rain hit, they felt the scrape of sand under the canoe's keel. It was hard to tell where the lake ended and land began. The squall descended like a giant fist, punching them with rain and wind so fierce it took their breath away.

Kiff felt it sting his bare back and raised a streaming face. Lightning suddenly lit the scene before him. The canoe had beached on one of the few sandy stretches along the west shore. The wall of tall poplars in front of them whipped back and forth in the gale force winds.

An instant later a fork of lightning struck a tree a few metres to their left. They heard the crack and groan as the tree fell. The smell of sulphur and burnt wood filled the air. With a mighty swoosh, the tree crashed into the water, its top branches brushing the side of the canoe.

"We've got to get out of here!" Josie screamed.
She scrambled out of the bow of the canoe.
Kiff and Dee hauled the shivering, terrified Drool
out of the bottom of the canoe and then all
four of them dragged it out of the water.

The rain changed to ice pellets. "Turn the canoe
over," Kiff yelled, running to get a driftwood
pole to prop up one side. They dived under
its shelter with Drool draped over their knees,
smelling of scared, wet dog.

For what seemed like hours, the lightning and
thunder flashed and cracked around them. Dark,
then light, then dark again. Hail drummed on
the canoe over their heads like a huge kettle

drum. It was impossible to hear anything, or see anything through the wall of rain.

And then, as fast as it had come, the squall blew over. The hail turned to a hard, steady rain. Through it, the beach appeared again, and the black lake turned a lighter shade of grey. The thunder rumbled in the distance, instead of crashing down around their heads.

They climbed out from under the canoe, shivering and exhausted. The big poplar blanketed the beach with its spreading branches. It had missed them by a metre! All of their clothes were soaked and dripping. Kiff's shirt was a wet rag, pinned under Drool's muddy paws.

"Look at him," Kiff laughed, trying to pull his shirt out from under the dog. "He's not going to budge." As Kiff yanked, Drool stiffly got to his feet, stretched under the canoe, and shook his wet fur all over them.

"Thanks, Drool," Kiff groaned. "I needed that."

"Listen!" Josie gripped his shoulder. "What's that noise?" Over the drumming of the rain on the canoe and the pounding of the waves, they could now hear a steady thumping, coming from the direction of the trees. Then a high-pitched, muffled whinny.

Kiff and Josie threw each other startled glances. "Sounds like a horse, kicking a van to bits, to me!" shouted Kiff. "We must be close to the road." He was off at a run with the others at his heels.

The dirt road around Big Pickle Lake ran just behind the screen of poplar trees. They reached it quickly. The storm had turned the road into a river of mud. Not far ahead through the steadily falling rain, they glimpsed the horse van, tipped at a crazy angle.

"Looks like they were trying to change a tire," Odie said. They could see a dark black shape leaning against the side of the van.

"Where are the louts?" Dee asked, trying to keep a grip on Drool's collar.

"They must be in the cab of the truck, waiting for the rain to stop," Kiff suggested.

"We have to do something," Josie said. "It sounds like Efstur is going nuts in there." The steady thumping continued. Ef was trying to kick his way out!

"Come on!" Kiff motioned them forward. "We'll open the back of the van, let them out, and two of us will ride away. Odie and I will do it. You and Dee run back to the canoe."

They spurted forward, being careful to stay directly behind the van so that they couldn't be seen in the truck's side mirrors.

But they had forgotten about Drool. He was glad to see the truck. It meant a chance of getting away from all this water. Trucks were good solid things to ride in, unlike tippy canoes. He trotted forward happily.

"Drool, come back!" Dee whispered frantically.

"They'll recognize him. They'll know we're here." Josie stopped short.

"We might have time ... " Kiff dashed forward, reached the van and twisted the handle on the back doors. But Drool was already leaping up at the window of the truck cab on the passenger side, wanting in.

They heard the door open, and Morley's surprised shout. "It's that big red dog again," he said. "How did he get here?"

Drool started his loud and noisy greeting. "Aroo-oo — " he howled.

"Change of plan," Kiff said quickly. "Get inside." All four of them scrambled into the horse van.

"Quiet, Ef. We're here," Kiff whispered, rubbing the chestnut horse under his frosty forelock to calm him. Efstur nuzzled into his shoulder and blew angrily through his nose, as if telling Kiff what a rough time he was having.

Josie heard a truck door slam. "I think they're coming. Get the door shut." Odie pulled the door behind him. There was no latch on the inside of the door, but he held it tight. They looked frantically around the small cramped space in the van. There was no time to hide.

"All right, all right, I'll check." It was Stan's voice they heard. Through the drumming of rain of the van's metal roof, they heard his footsteps squish toward the back of the van. They braced themselves for the door to swing open.

"Never mind," they heard Morley call back. "That crazy little horse has stopped kicking." They held their breaths, waiting. "You see those kids out there?"

"No kids, Morley," Stan shouted. "The dog must have run ahead of them ... " There was a pause. He was just a thin wall of aluminum away. "It's still raining too blinkin' hard to change that tire." Then they heard Stan's footsteps squish back through the mud to the pickup. They heard the door open and slam behind him.

"Whew!" Kiff grinned at the other three faces in the dim van. "That was close!"

"What are we going to do now?" Dee asked. "And where's Drool?"

"If I know your dog, he's warming up in the cab, listening to country music with the boys, and getting nice and dry, " Kiff said. "We're going back to the original plan. Let's get Smoke and Efstur out of here!"

10

Locked In

"But we can't leave Drool with those guys!" Dee said in dismay. Kiff was already undoing the ropes that held Smoke firmly to the sides of the van.

"Not again," Kiff groaned. "We can't take Drool. We can't leave Drool. That dog of yours is a four-legged, four-star pain!"

"They might hurt him if we get away on the horses," Dee argued.

"I might hurt him if we don't!" Kiff muttered, with the loose rope in his hand.

"Be quiet, they're coming back!" Josie hissed.

Stan and Morley were arguing fiercely about who was going to change the tire and who was going to check the horses. "I don't want to get kicked in the face!" Stan yelled.

"You think changing this tire is easy?" Morley hollered back. "This van weighs a ton."

"Pair of lazy cowards!" Josie muttered.

"Down," Kiff ordered. "Under the straw." He wiggled past Smoke's bulk and dived head first into the pile of loose straw in the front of the van. He made a hole for Dee in the straw beside him, covered her head loosely in the dry, prickly stalks, then buried himself. They could hear Josie and Odie rustling in the straw on the floor of the van, then the door swung open, letting in the light.

"Good thing I checked," Stan called. "This door wasn't latched ... looks like that rope on the big fellow got undone," he muttered, and they felt the floor lurch as he took a step into the van. He heard Dee gasp beside him. They'd get stepped on — discovered!

Just then Efstur let out a wild whinny and lashed out with his rear hooves. Stan gave a sharp cry, slammed the door shut, and drove home the latch.

"Nice work, Ef," Kiff breathed. "Saved by a whinny!"

"We're locked in ... " Kiff could hear Odie whisper in the darkness. "I don't call that *saved*."

Stan had gone to help Morley jack up the van.

"Raise it easy!" Stan urged. "We don't want to spook the horses and start them kicking again."

"Why don't you jack it up, if you don't like the way I'm doing it," Morley panted. "It feels even heavier than it was before the storm!"

Inside, they could feel the side of the van tip a little higher each time Morley cranked the jack. It must be hard work with the four of us and two horses to lift, Kiff thought. Good. He didn't have any kind feelings towards those two thugs. When the time came to get even, he was going to enjoy it!

"I hate this … " Dee murmured beside him. "I have claustrophobia."

"Shh! Listen," Kiff grabbed her arm. "They're talking about Drool."

"What are we going to do with him?" Stan was saying. "I didn't bargain for no big dog on my lap."

The four hidden passengers stuffed their wet sleeves in their mouths to keep from giggling out loud. The picture of Stan in the passenger seat with Drool draped all over him was too funny.

"Take him along," Morley said. "I'll bet he's worth a buck or two to somebody — maybe one of those labs — you know, where they do animal experiments?"

"No!" Dee cried.

"I didn't bargain to steal no dog ... " Stan muttered again.

"We're not stealing him," Morley pointed out. "He's a lost dog, and we picked him up, that's all. He wanted to get in the truck, didn't he? He loves sitting on your lap, doesn't he? The main thing is to get these horses down to Tackle Bay and get them sold at that auction," Morley went on. "If we hang around here much longer, those kids are going to come along and make trouble."

"I think we should stay off of the highway," Stan grunted. "This rear axle doesn't look too good." They could rear him banging something underneath them.

"Just hurry up," Morley said. "We've wasted enough time with this flat and the storm."

"What do you think I'm doing here, squatting down in this mud for fun?" They could hear Stan grunt as he tightened each nut on the tire. "There. All done."

"This van *is* a wreck," Odie whispered. "I can see right out through a crack over here. The rivets are all sprung in this seam. Right now, Stan's covered in mud, and Morley is a clean as a whistle. They're getting back in the truck."

"Can you see Drool?" Dee whispered.

"No, he must still be in the cab," Odie told her.

They heard the truck motor start, then a lurch as the van rolled forward. The two horses stood quietly, comforted by their voices. Kiff stood up, shedding straw and tightened Smoke's ropes again as they bounced and swayed over the ruts.

"I've got an idea," Josie said, picking the straw out of her long, dark hair. "They'll have to stop somewhere — for gas or at a stop sign. We can yell and bang on the walls for help."

"It's worth a try," Odie agreed, "if we stop."

As it turned out, they stopped sooner than anyone imagined. The truck jolted suddenly to a halt just a few kilometres down the road. They heard truck doors bang, cursing, and another argument.

"It's a *big* tree, Stan, " Morley groaned. "We're never going to lift it!"

They took a chance on looking out the van window. The two men were trying to lift a monster pine that had been struck by lightning. It had fallen across the road, blocking their path.

"We'll have to cut it, Morley," Stan said, kicking the solid trunk.

"We don't have a saw, Stan," Morley said.

Drool had hopped out of the cab to take a look. When he saw that the two men were just going to *stand* there, looking at the tree, he lost interest and came sniffing around the van.

"Aroo-oo!" he howled, as he caught Dee's scent, and then barked, jumping at the back door and scratching at the aluminum with his claws.

"What's up with that fool dog?" Morley came striding over. The four ducked down quickly from the window. They peered out through the crack in the seam.

"He must smell the horses, Morley," Stan said. "Why don't we let him in there, with them?"

"Yes!" whispered Dee, fiercely.

"No!" Kiff said, equally fierce. "He'll see us when he opens the door!"

"Why don't we leave well enough alone," Morley advised. "The horses are all peaceful. If you open that door you're likely to get kicked again."

That argument made sense to Stan. They heard him squelch back to the fallen pine tree. "Well, what are we gonna do?"

"We'll turn around," Morley said. "What time is the auction?"

Stan was uncurling a long piece of paper that he had rolled into a cylinder with an elastic around it. "It says tonight at seven, and tomorrow at nine," Stan said.

"There's a back road to Tackle Bay that runs off this one up by the junction," Morley nodded. "We can still make it tonight."

"So that's where we're going — a horse auction!" Kiff breathed.

"I saw that poster in the hotel," Odie said. "The auction is at Tackle Bay."

They heard the truck motor start up again a few minutes later and grind into reverse. The horse van leaned and swayed and jolted as Morley tried to turn the rig around on the narrow road.

"Man," Odie said. "Listen to that engine." Both Odie and Kiff spent a lot of time around engines at the farm and fishing camp. They knew when one was on its last legs.

"And there goes our idea of yelling for help," Kiff groaned. "There's probably nothing but moose and bears between here and Tackle Bay on that back road.

"Moose and bears? Really?" Dee sounded nervous.

"We'll have to be ready for anything," Josie said. She was braced against the wall of the van as they bucketed from side to side on the rough road. "When that back door opens, we need to have a plan ready."

11

The Road to Tackle Bay

The rain had punched potholes in the road. The old van bumped and creaked along, throwing the passengers inside back and forth. Even Smoke complained, raising his silver head to whinny and stamping his hoof in the straw.

After the four friends made their plan, there was nothing to do on the long journey, but talk and sing songs with lots of verses.

They sang "There's a Hole in My Bucket" and "Ninety-nine Bottles of Beer on the Wall." Then they named all their cousins — first and last names. Dee had the most — twenty-four first cousins.

"That must be neat," Kiff said. "Like having lots of brothers and sisters." He looked over at Josie, swaying and jolting in the shadows. "Did you ever think, Moonbrain, that you and I and Odie are all only kids?"

"That's why I get stuck with you," Josie said, "every summer."

"Don't start," Odie groaned. "This horse van is too small and too smelly to put up with you two fighting."

"Shouldn't we be rehearsing our plan?" Dee suggested.

"I can't rehearse on an empty stomach!" Kiff groaned. "Do you realize how long it is since we had anything to eat?"

"Kiff," Josie explained to Dee, "has never missed a meal in his life."

"Well, it has been a long time since breakfast," Dee said. "I'm so hungry I could eat a ... "

"Horse?" Kiff asked, and they all laughed. But it wasn't funny, and they knew it.

"It won't hurt to go over the plan," Odie suggested. "It might even get Kiff's mind off his stomach."

"All right," Kiff sighed. "We all hide in the straw when we get to the outskirts of town. "When the doors open we dive forward, making as much noise as we can ... "

Just then there was a terrible thump, the van lurched to one side, and for an awful moment seemed like it was going to tip over. Kiff and the others hurled themselves against the high side. The horses neighed in terror as the broken van bumped down the road a few more metres and then stopped.

"Get ready," Kiff hissed and the four of them dived for the floor, burrowing into the straw once more.

They heard the pickup's doors slam, and footsteps plodding back on both sides of the van.

"Come over here," Morley's voice rang out from underneath them. "The blasted back axle's completely broken."

"Now what?" Stan sounded exhausted.

"Get that dog's tail out of my face!" Morley shouted. They could hear scuffling and happy growling noises somewhere under them.

"He's not my dog!" Stan said.

"Just get him out of here," Morley growled. "We've got a big problem, Stan. We can't haul this horse van with a broken axle. And we're out here in the back of beyond without tools." Morley gave the van a kick that rattled all their bones and swore loudly for several minutes.

"Well, the truck's still running," Stan said, hopefully.

"Yeah, and we're getting in it and driving back to Pickle Lake," Morley said in a voice of decision. "I'm thirsty. I need a beer to clear my head."

"We're just going to leave these horses out here in the van?"

"Yeah. Come on."

"How about the dog?"

"Leave him too!"

"But he'll starve to death out here ... " They could hear Drool whining as he danced around the two men.

"Use your brain, Stan. That dog is like a red flag. Everybody in town knows he belongs to those people with the Jeep."

"Aw beans," Stan finally said. "I was really looking forward to that horse auction at Tackle Bay. I've got that neat poster rolled up in the truck and I could just picture us, standing by the rail while they bid on our fine horses ... "

"*Your* fine horses," Kiff whispered in a furious voice. "You've got a lot of nerve!"

"Come on, Stan. I'm really thirsty," Morley was already walking toward the truck.

"But these poor old horses are going to starve too, before anybody finds them. And what's Bruce going to say when he finds out we borrowed his van and didn't bring it back?"

"Who says he's going to find out ... " They were still arguing when the truck door slammed and they rattled away.

There was a hush inside the van.

"I don't believe they just left us here ... locked in," Dee said at last. "I have to go to the bathroom," she whispered to Josie.

They could hear Drool whining softly outside. "It's okay Drool. We're here," Kiff yelled, and Drool burst into a frenzy of happy barking and howling.

"Odie, that crack where the rivets popped," Josie shouted over Drool's noise. "Do you think we could make it bigger?"

"If we had a crowbar, or something to use as a lever, maybe," Odie said.

They looked around the inside of the van. The grey square of light from the small window was getting dimmer. It was hard to see. At last Odie found a thick piece of wood on the floor under the straw.

"Good work," Josie said. "Let's try it."

Kiff and Odie leaned against the loose panel. They shoved it out far enough for Dee and Josie to thrust in the end of the thick board. Then all four leaned on it with all their strength.

The rivets popped like pistol shots going off in the wilderness quiet. "That does it," Odie grinned. "You go first, Dee. You're the thinnest."

"Watch the edges of the metal," Kiff said, as Dee squirmed through the gap. She was met by a dog beside himself with joy. As each one emerged from the van Drool licked their faces, slobbered on their hands, and cried and whined with pleasure to see them again.

They stood on the muddy road at last, looking in the direction the truck had disappeared.

"Well," said Kiff, "anybody know where we are?"

12

Abandoned

Josie, Dee, and Odie all shook their heads. One wilderness road looked pretty much like another. Tall, dark evergreens closed in on both sides. Up ahead the road curved through rock, blasted with dynamite by the road builders.

"I don't think we turned off the main road," Josie said at last. "But we don't know how far it is back to town. We should have been paying more attention, instead of singing Kiff's stupid songs!"

"Oh sure, blame it all on me," Kiff said.

Suddenly Dee started to laugh. "Look at us," she chuckled. "Just look at us. We're all alone, and we're hungry and thirsty and tired and ... just ... look at us!"

Kiff, Odie and Josie looked at her in shock, and then at each other. Bits of straw were stuck in their hair. Kiff and Odie were in muddy riding boots, Josie and Dee in muddy shoes. Kiff's shirt was a rag that might have been blue a long time ago, and the rest of their clothes were damp and dirty from the storm and long hours in the van.

They all started to laugh. Drool thought this was great. He howled and looped in the air and wiggled in all directions at once. "Hold him," Dee choked at last. "I have to make a run for the bushes."

"Here, Drool," Kiff picked up a stick from the ditch by the side of the road. "Go fetch." He flung it in the opposite direction from Dee, and Drool raced after it, happy to be chasing a stick.

"Good dog," Kiff said. "Now bring it back!" But Drool, of course, would not bring the stick back. He gripped it in his teeth and danced just out of reach when Kiff tried to grab it.

"I'm going to teach him to fetch a stick if it's the last thing I do," Kiff laughed.

Just then there was an impatient neigh from the back of the van.

"The poor horses," Josie cried. "We've got to let them out."

They turned to the ruined van. "Poor Bruce, whoever he is," Kiff shook his head. "I don't think he'd recognize this wreck!"

The van door was unlatched, the ropes undone and the two horses were soon munching long grass at the side of the road.

"Ohhh!" groaned Kiff. "I could eat grass. Or bark and leaves, like a beaver, I'm so hungry."

"What are we going to do?" Dee asked.

"I think the best idea is to ride back in the direction of town," Josie said, looking down the long road.

"But there's only two horses, and four of us ... " Dee looked doubtfully at little Efstur, who was not much taller than a pony.

"Don't worry about Ef," Kiff said. "Horses like him carry huge men in Iceland all day long. Smoke will get tired before he does." Efstur shook his shaggy mane as if to agree with Kiff.

"We'll each have to ride behind one of the guys, because they have the riding boots." Josie wrinkled her nose at the idea. "I'll go with Odie on Smoke."

"Good!" Kiff said. "I'd rather ride with a boa constrictor than you, Moon!"

"Well, I'd rather ride with a wart hog ... "

Odie was blushing furiously. He turned away and pretended to be busy cinching up Smoke's saddle, but they could all see the tips of his bright red ears.

Kiff's face filled with glee. "Of course Odie is *jumping for joy* to be riding with *Josie*," he crowed. "Aren't you Odie?"

"Dry up, Kokatow," Odie mumbled. "Didn't you say you were hungry or something? Let's go." Odie swung up on Smoke's high saddle and reached out his hand to help Josie on behind him.

"Your face is going to burn out, if you blush like that all the way back," Kiff laughed.

Kiff threw his leg over Efstur's broad back, and Dee climbed up awkwardly behind him. "Are you okay?" he asked over his shoulder.

"I think so," Dee said. She clutched Kiff around the waist. "It feels like I might slip off … "

Kiff felt a bit odd with Dee holding onto him like that. I didn't know girls' hair tickled like that, he thought. But I won't blush. Odie would get too much satisfaction, and Josie would never let me forget it! I won't blush. I won't.

"We should get going," Josie glanced down at him from her seat behind Odie. "It's going to get dark soon." They could not see the sun through the thick layer of grey clouds, but the light was fading.

"My parents will be worried if I'm not home before dark!" Dee cried.

"All our parents will be worried," Josie agreed, "especially if they find my canoe drifting!"

Drool seemed to know how to run with the horses without getting tangled in their feet. He kept just ahead, sometimes dashing off to the side to check the ditch for interesting smells, but never crossing in front of them.

"I didn't know the fool dog had that much sense in him, " Kiff said.

"He doesn't mean to make trouble," Dee sighed. "He just gets carried away."

Kiff laughed. "You can say that again." Even hungry, tired, cold, and with a girl behind him, it felt good to be riding again. The road seemed to go on forever, around a bend, straight, around another bend. It was all getting kind of blurred.

"Wait a second!" Dee jabbed him in the ribs and sat up straight. "Stop, Kiff."

13

A Familiar Corner

"Whoa, boy." Kiff gently pulled back on the reins. "What is it?"

"That road back there, the one we just passed... " Dee's voice shook with excitement.

"You mean that little track on the left?"

"Yes. Can we go back?"

Odie and Josie, up ahead, had stopped and were looking back at them.

"Dee wants to go back," Kiff called. "She says something looks familiar." He shrugged. Dee must be hallucinating, he thought. Lack of food. Low blood sugar.

"I knew it." She leaned around his shoulder for a better look. "This is the turn-off. We stopped here once because the blueberries were just too big and gorgeous to pass by. Remember, Drool?"

Drool had run back to the culvert over the ditch and was sniffing the tire tracks with great interest. He whined eagerly.

"Blueberries?" Kiff came out of his fog. "Blueberries you say? Where?"

"I don't know if any are left," Dee hurried on. "But that doesn't matter. Kiff! This is where my parents have been coming every day to work. This is the trail to Fort James!"

"It is?" Kiff looked down the trail. It disappeared into the thick dark forest of jack pines, like a thousand other trails in these woods. "I don't see any marker or anything. Are you sure?"

"There isn't a marker!" Dee said. "They don't want people poking their noses into the dig."

"What is it?" Odie and Josie trotted up on Smoke.

"Dee says this track leads to Fort James," Kiff told them. "And *blueberries*, which is more important."

"There might still be some workers down at the dig," Dee said eagerly. "Maybe even my parents."

"How far is it?" Odie asked. He didn't want to dampen Dee's enthusiasm, but if the dig was far, they might be wasting precious time and energy to get there.

"It's hard to say," Dee admitted. "I've only gone by truck."

"What do we have to lose?" Kiff said. "We're not going to make it back to town before dark anyway." The thought of bypassing blueberries was just too hard. Even a handful, to keep his stomach from totally collapsing!

"All right," Josie agreed. "But let's hurry."

The road to Fort James was just a dirt track, with grass in the middle, and bare rock in many places. In the dim light under the pines, the horses picked their way slowly. The track led downwards through the trees, and the forest was so still, so weirdly silent, that they could hear every sound of the horses' feet and their own breathing.

"There," Dee finally said. "Around the next bend." The forest opened up, and water shone silver under the grey sky.

"I don't see any fort." Kiff was disappointed.

"It's just holes in the ground," Dee explained. "They're digging up where the fort used to be."

"There's no one here," Josie scanned the clearing. They all felt a sinking, desperate feeling. The wall of silent trees behind them and the long muddy road seemed too hard to retrace. Without saying a word, Kiff slid off his saddle and the other three followed.

"The blueberries are dried up," Kiff kicked at a low green bush. "I didn't see one nice plump juicy one the whole way in here."

Kiff couldn't keep the despair out of his voice. It had sounded so exciting — an old fort on the shores of a lake. Instead there was a bleak, rain-soaked clearing and nothing to eat. He sank down on a log bench beside a stone fire pit and stirred the wet ashes with a stick. "So this is the fabulous fort."

"I knew it wouldn't mean anything to you, Kokatow," Josie said. "That's why I didn't want you to come." She turned and scanned the forest with eager eyes. "There used to be a native encampment somewhere near the fort too."

The horses had gone down to the lake to drink, and Drool followed, standing in the water for a long, satisfying slurp. This was the kind of water he liked. No slippery dock, no treacherous, jagged rocks. A dog could just wade out into the soft shallow mud and drink all he wanted! Drool came sloshing back and drooled lovingly on each of them.

"Thanks Drool," Josie said. "That's exactly what I needed — a handful of dog slime." She wiped her fingers on her jeans and walked down to the water to get the horses.

"Too bad it's too cold to go swimming," Kiff eyed the calm, inviting lake. "It would feel good after all that mud and prickly straw."

"Not me!" Dee shivered. "I've never been so cold and wet in my life. I'm going to help Josie. Moving is better than just sitting here."

Kiff looked after her. "If we just had some matches," he said, poking the fire pit, "I could make a big roaring fire and she'd get warm fast enough!"

"What's this?" Odie teased. "Kiff Kokatow to the rescue? I never thought I'd see the day when you cared if a girl froze to death!"

"Oh, go kick a stump," Kiff grunted. How had things turned out this way, he wondered. He was supposed to be teasing Odie, not the other way around. After all, Dee was from the city. She wasn't used to roughing it like they were. "C'mon," he growled. "Let's go help tie up the horses."

"What's that?" Odie pointed to a flash of white behind some brush, as they tied Smoke and Efstur in a safe, sheltered spot.

"Oh that's the supply trailer," Dee said.

"Supplies?" Kiff shook off his black mood. "What kind of supplies, Dee?"

"Oh, you know, stuff for the dig like shovels and picks and photography supplies and blankets and food and ... " Dee's voice trailed off and her eyes became enormous. "I think I can remember the combination on the lock!"

They all started to run. Drool found a stick and dashed at Kiff, hoping they were going to play a chasing game, but all Kiff could think about was that magic word — food!

14

Noises in the Dark

A few minutes later, the door swung outwards, and they all crowded into the trailer. It was dim, but brighter than the horse trailer, with windows letting in light from both sides.

"Is there food in those boxes?" Kiff pointed to a neat stack of plastic bins.

"No," Dee laughed. "That's the stuff they've dug up — the artifacts from the fort."

"Where would they keep the food?" Kiff said impatiently. "The food, Dee, and the matches!"

"I'm trying to remember," Dee said. "Maybe that metal cupboard."

Kiff twisted the metal handles and threw open the cupboard doors. There was a sigh of delight from four famished throats. Pop cans, boxes of granola bars and raisins, plastic baggies full of trail mix and nuts crammed the shelves.

"Who does all this belong to?" Odie's eyes were huge. "Would they mind?"

"Would they deny food to starving children?" Kiff rolled his eyes. "Of course not." He reached for a bag of peanuts and started stuffing them in his mouth.

"It's food for the workers," Dee said. "I'm sure Kiff is right. If they knew how hungry we are ... " She reached for a box of granola bars. "I'm sure it's all right. Who wants one?"

"What's this?" Kiff was exploring the shelves. He held up a clear plastic bag full of something that looked like dried mud and string. "Fish bait?"

"That's a dried dinner," Dee explained, munching on a nut and oatmeal bar. She took the bag and read the label. "'Spaghetti with Tomato Sauce.' We just need to add water and heat it up."

"Forget it!" Kiff laughed. "I wouldn't feed this to Drool! Who eats this stuff?"

"The workers do," Dee said. "But you have to boil it for a while to soften it up, I think."

"We need a fire, anyway," Josie was feeling the shelves over her head. "They probably have matches in waterproof cans. Here!" Triumphantly she pulled off a lid and showed them a can full of beautiful dry wood matches.

The matches were dry, but the woods were wet from a day of rain. They searched up and down the lakefront for dry driftwood, twisted dead balsam branches off the bottoms of trees, and peeled white bark off dead birch trunks.

Half an hour later, they were warming themselves in front of a blazing fire.

By now, it was dark in the clearing. Kiff had dragged a small dead balsam fir near the fire pit and was feeding handfuls of dried needles to the fire to keep it burning hotly. The sparks drifted up in the night air, and the flames lit their faces with a reddish glow.

"It's a great fire," Dee sighed happily.

"Yup," Kiff grinned. "You could cook anything on that fire — if you had anything to cook."

"If we just had some hot dogs," Odie agreed, "and buns, and marshmallows."

"We could try the fish worm dinner," Kiff said. "Who knows? It might even taste good."

They found a pot in the supply trailer, a big round kettle with a black bottom that the workers had used to boil water for coffee. Odie filled it with lake water, while Kiff and Dee built up the fire and Josie rummaged in the trailer for bowls for the spaghetti. The darkness was almost complete. Only a faint glow in the sky to the west marked where the sun had set over the lake. Josie had found a powerful flashlight in the trailer and they could see her light bobbing around through the open door.

"Do you think we'll have to stay all night?" Dee asked.

Kiff poked a big piece of driftwood into the heart of the fire. A shower of sparks went up. "Don't worry," he said. "We'll be all right here.

I saw some tarps in the trailer, and there are coats to cover us."

"I'm worried about my mom and dad," Dee said. "They must have waited here for us all day, and when we didn't come, they must have thought the canoe tipped or something terrible happened to us."

"I know," Kiff nodded. "All of our parents will be worried." He gazed into the fire, thinking of the scene at Camp Kokatow, especially if they had found Josie's canoe drifting upside down. "They'll probably figure out we're together when Odie and I and the horses don't come back," he tried to reassure Dee. "And they know we can look after ourselves in the woods."

Josie's swinging flashlight beam came towards the fire pit. "I found three muddy bowls," she said. "It looks like they used them to clean artifacts from the fort. I'd better rinse them out in the lake." Her flashlight bobbed away towards the water.

Drool came dashing out of the dark, all wet paws and slobber, and thrust himself in between them. Kiff laughed. "He thinks this is just a big adventure."

"He's never had granola bars for dinner," Dee said. "Lie down, Drool. You're getting me all wet again!"

But Drool was already racing back to greet Odie and Josie with the full pot of water and clean bowls. "And now for the great experi-

ment," Odie said. "Will this disgusting package of goop turn into dinner before our very eyes?"

"Or will Drool have a new taste treat?" Kiff finished. He fished the hard dry mass of twisted noodles and sauce out of the bag and tossed it in the pot.

"Wait," Dee shouted, "that's too much water!"

She was right. Half an hour later they were trying to eat something that looked like spaghetti soup.

"At least it's hot," Josie sighed. "Kokatow, why can't you ever think before you do something?"

"How was I supposed to know how much water?" Kiff said, putting his bowl down so

Drool could lap up the rest. The setter made happy slurping sounds in the dark.

"Keep him quiet!" Odie said suddenly. "I heard something."

By the time they'd got Drool to stop drinking the spaghetti juice, the sound of a truck coming down the track was very clear.

"It could be Stan and Morley, looking for the horses!" Kiff said. "We've got to hide!"

"Throw the spaghetti on the fire," Josie said quickly. "If they see the fire they'll know we're here."

Quickly the kettle was dumped over the glowing coals, and blackness settled on the clearing like a thick mat. Josie cupped her hand over the flashlight's beam, and they ran to where Efstur and Smoke were standing quietly in the trees.

"Let's get them behind the supply trailer," Odie suggested. "Quiet, big girl," he told Smoke as he untied her and led her into the woods. Kiff followed with Efstur.

They could hear the truck getting close, changing to a lower gear as it came down the last slope to the clearing. Josie switched off her light completely, and they waited.

"They'll smell the spaghetti!" Dee hissed.

It was true. A faint scent of garlic and oregano hung in the air.

"Maybe they won't get out of the truck if they don't see a light," Kiff said. But at that moment they heard two truck doors slam. The sound was like pistol shots in the still night air.

All four of them held their breath. Kiff had his hand on Efstur's soft muzzle, warning him to be quiet. If a flea sneezed, he thought, you'd hear him in this silence.

"Nothing here," came a voice. "I guess we'd better get this truck back to town."

Four tense, listening bodies relaxed. But they had forgotten about Drool. At the sound of the man's voice, he wriggled out of Dee's grip and dashed off through the brush, whining happily in his throat.

"Oh, no!" Kiff groaned under his breath. That useless fool of a dog! He was going to give them away, again!

15

Just Get Those Guys!

"Drool, come back," he heard Dee whisper in the darkness, but of course she might as well have been calling back a river rushing over a waterfall. They could hear the sounds of a scuffle, and sharp cries of fear and alarm. Over it all was Drool's joyful "Aroo-oo" of greeting and then an astonished female voice.

"It's all right, Neil. It's a dog, not a wolf!"

"I know that voice!" Dee exclaimed, throwing herself forward. "Josie, give me the light! It's me ... Dee!" she shouted.

"What are you doing?" Kiff sputtered, trying to hold her back.

"Kiff, that's Amy. She's one of the Fort James workers!"

Then they all stumbled over each other to get out into the clearing. The two workers shone their flashlights in their faces, making it harder to run. Drool dashed in and out around their legs. "It's Drool!" the girl called Amy shouted.

"And Dee and her friends. One, two, three, four. They're all here!"

"What have you been cooking?" Neil sniffed the air. "It smells like burned pizza."

"We tried your dried spaghetti," Dee explained. "But we drowned it."

"Well, I'm just glad it wasn't you who drowned," Amy said. "Your parents have been frantic, Dee. We've been combing the countryside for you."

"I'm sorry," Dee said. "What made you come back here?"

"Amy wanted to check the site one last time," Neil explained. "I said let's go back to town, but she claimed she was getting psychic messages that you were somewhere close by." Neil looked wet and tired.

"The messages were probably from Drool," Amy said, ruffling his ears. "Dogs are very psychic." She looked hard at the four of them. "You're going to be in big trouble with your parents, you know. Were you planning to camp out here all night or something?"

"You guys don't understand," Dee tried to explain. "There wasn't any plan. We've had this really totally awful day."

"We have to get the police," Kiff broke in. "Some guys tried to steal our horses."

Neil's eyebrow shot up beneath the brim of his hat. "Police?"

"Stan and Morley kidnapped our horses," Kiff said again. "The horse van broke down on the road to Tackle Bay, and we got away ... " He could see by the looks on Neil and Amy's face that he wasn't making any sense.

"Josie, you and Dee go back and tell all our parents we're okay," he said. "Odie and I will stay here with the horses. And make sure Stan and Morley don't leave town."

"We can't leave you here," Amy said, looking around the dark clearing.

"We'll build up the fire again, and wait for you to come back with a horse van," Kiff said. "If you can't get one tonight, we'll ride back to town in the morning." He shrugged. "I'm not leaving the horses again."

"Me neither," Odie agreed. "Our folks will understand. Kiff and I have slept out in the bush lots of times."

Amy looked at their worried faces. "Okay," she finally agreed. "We won't waste any more time arguing. The most important thing is to let everybody know you're safe."

"Are you sure you don't want me to stay?" Josie asked Kiff.

"No, you should go," Odie said quickly. "Tell them about what happened. They know you always tell the truth. Kiff and I ..." He stopped, looking embarrassed.

"Thanks a lot," Kiff looked disgusted. "What a pal you are, Odie."

"You have been known to make up some incredible stories," Josie shook her head. "All right. Dee and I will go. But we'll come back if we find a van tonight."

"Just get Stan and Morley," Kiff said. "That's all I care about!"

"We'll have to leave the dog," Neil said. "There's no room in the truck with four of us in the cab."

"I'll leave Drool to look after you," Dee said. At the sound of his name, Drool sat up straight, ready to be praised.

"Oh thanks," Kiff groaned. "He'll be an enormous comfort."

Drool was unhappy about being left behind, but even if Dee had wanted to take him, there was no room in the cab. Drool would have run after the pickup if Kiff hadn't wrestled him to the ground and hung on as the truck bounced away up the track.

Amy and Neil had left them their two powerful flashlights to light the clearing. But the fire pit was drenched with spaghetti water and they had to start a fire from scratch on the wet ashes. Kiff tore the birch bark into tiny strips and mixed it with balsam needles. Then he built a small teepee of balsam twigs over the ball of needles and bark.

He struck a match, and the little teepee burst into flame. He and Odie carefully fed it small sticks, each one a little larger until the fire was blazing hot enough for a chunk of driftwood. The driftwood knots burned best and longest, and soon they had a warm blaze going again. Their faces reflected the firelight as they sat close, feeding sticks to the flames.

"Think they'll be back?" Kiff asked.

"You mean the girls? Tonight?"

"Forget the girls!" Kiff stirred the fire angrily. "I meant do you think that somebody will come back for us and the horses?"

"Maybe. Who else has a horse van in town besides Bruce?"

"Your grandfather will know. Somebody has to have a van. We have to get out of here." Kiff gave the fire a savage poke. "I just want to give Stan and Morley a little piece of what's coming to them!"

Drool whined anxiously and flopped down close beside Kiff. He didn't like being separated from Dee, and he was hungry. The granola bars had only stimulated his great doggy appetite, not satisfied it.

"I know what you mean, buddy," Kiff groaned. "I'm starving too."

16

Sneezing Beans

Dee and Josie bounced along in the truck back to town, squashed between Amy, at the wheel, and Neil, staring out the window at the darkness. Josie felt too tired to raise her voice above the growl of the engine. She tried to think about all that had happened that day, but it seemed a blur.

Certain moments stood out. Watching the canoe float away down the lake. Stan and Morley stealing the horses. The storm. Hiding in the horse van. She would have to try to remember it all clearly. They were going to have a lot of explaining to do!

"Do you think the guys will be all right?" Dee whispered in her ear.

"Of course. What's going to happen to them out there!" Josie hissed back.

"I don't know. I thought maybe bears or more horse thieves."

"We don't have that many bears or crooks roaming the woods," Josie couldn't help chuckling. From Dee's short experience, Big Pickle Lake must seem like a pretty dangerous place.

"I hated to leave Kiff and Odie there, after all we've been through together," Dee sighed.

Josie poked her hard with her elbow. "What do you mean?" she demanded. "Kiff and Odie got us into all this trouble. If they hadn't ridden after us ... "

"But Kiff did rescue us with his canoe!" Dee's voice was rising.

"He only *had* the canoe because he wanted to follow us!"

Their argument had got Neil's attention. He turned and grinned at them. "Still thinking about those boys, are you?" he teased. "I'm sorry we had to break up your cozy campfire."

"You don't know what you're talking about," Josie said angrily. She glared at Neil in the dark cab. But she couldn't blame him for what he said. The way Dee went on about Kiff, you'd think he was a hero or something! Instead of a menace. Nosey parker. Butt-in-ski. Weirdo! Josie entertained herself with thinking up nasty names for Kiff Kokatow the rest of the way to town.

* * *

Back at Fort James, Kiff and Odie were finally filling their stomachs with hot food.

"The mistake I made," Odie said with his mouth full, "was letting you talk me into the stupid idea of riding after the girls and cutting them off at the portage!"

"And the mistake *I* made," Kiff shot back, "was letting you talk me into getting so worried about old Moonbrain and Dee that I left the horses!" He shook his head as he scraped his plate empty. "Is there any more?'

"No," Odie said. "I gave the rest to Drool." They had found another package of dried dinner, brown and lumpy. When heated up with water, it turned out to be vegetarian chili — and pretty good, too. The boys each had huge plates, and Odie had turned the pot over to Drool. He was not pleased with the chili pepper and kept sneezing as he slurped it down.

"Drool! You just sneezed a bean in my ear!" Kiff cried. "Did you ever see such a useless dog! Go eat someplace else."

"Don't pretend you don't like him," Odie said. "And you like Dee, too. I don't see why you always have to act like you don't." His face was thoughtful in the dancing flames. "Maybe you're afraid to admit it."

Kiff kicked a log that was falling out of the fire. Sparks shot into the night sky. "I didn't say I didn't like Drool," he growled. "I said he was useless. What has he done all day except get us into trouble? And now he's spitting beans at me."

Drool thought Kiff had got up to play a game. He growled happily and danced around Kiff's legs. "You've got to admit," Kiff laughed, "that he's not too bright! Beautiful, but not bright."

"Beautiful ... " Odie said. "Like Dee."

"If you don't stop talking about *girls* I'm going to throw you in the lake," Kiff said. "But first let's check on the horses. Then we should see if there's anything in the trailer to make a bed. It looks like we might be here all night!"

The powerful flashlights Amy and Neil had given them threw two strong paths of light towards the trees where they had tied Smoke and Efstur. Drool danced in and out of the flashlights' beams, sniffing all the exciting night smells.

The two horses were standing peacefully. Smoke rested her big head on Efstur's shaggy one. "Looks like they'll be fine till morning," Kiff said. "Let's check out the trailer."

Inside, they stood the flashlights on opposite shelves so they lit the small space. Under the shelves and table were deep pools of blackness, but they could see their way around.

"Let's take a look in those stacking bins," Kiff said. "I want to see what they're digging up."

"I don't think we should touch anything ... " Odie warned, but it was too late. Kiff was already lifting the lid off the top bin.

"Just some old square-head nails and junk," Kiff sighed. "Practically all rust." He put that bin to one side and peered into the next. "This looks more interesting."

"If you wreck this stuff, we're going to be in major trouble," Odie warned. "Let's just find some blankets and get out of here."

"It's already wrecked," Kiff said. "These are just pieces of broken dishes. They must have dug up a kitchen!" He pulled off the next bin. "Wow, look Odie, an old gun!"

He stood up, holding an ancient pistol. "BANG BANG!" he shouted.

At Kiff's sudden shout Drool gave a mighty leap into the stack of bins. It crashed to the floor of the trailer, spilling the contents of ten carefully packed collections of precious artifacts in all directions.

There was terrible silence in the trailer, except for Drool's excited panting, and the swish of his tail.

"I really can't believe you did that," Odie said in a hollow voice.

"I *didn't!*" Kiff protested. "It was Drool! Of all the stupid ... Help me Odie. We've got to get all this stuff back in the right bins. Drool, let go of that, that ... " He stared at Odie. "What is that he's got in his mouth?"

Drool had found a bone. It was a very old bone, but being a dog, he wasn't fussy.

17

Old Bones

"DROOL!" bellowed Kiff in a terrible voice, "BRING ME BACK THAT BONE!"

But Drool, of course, did not. He bounced away with the bone in his mouth, daring Kiff to come after him and take it. Kiff made a dive, but Drool twisted away, as if to say, "You'll never catch me." More boxes crashed in the crowded trailer.

"We've got to get that bone," Kiff shouted. "What if it's a priceless treasure?"

"What if it's a human bone?" Odie said, making a dive at Drool from the other direction. He and Kiff landed on the trailer floor, face to face, while Drool leaped over their heads and out the trailer door.

"Do you really think it could be ... human?" Kiff's face was pale in the flashlight beam. "Come on!" He scrambled to his feet.

"You know you'll never catch him," Odie groaned. "That dumb dog could hide the bone in the brush. Bury it on the beach. Chew it up!"

"We've got to get it!" Kiff said again. He grabbed one flashlight and tore after Drool.

Odie was still on his hands and knees. He picked up the other flashlight and shone it on one of the bins and read the label. It had numbers. He rummaged through the bits of rusty nails and hinges, glass and pottery on the floor and noticed that each one also had a number on a tag attached.

"Odie!" Kiff stuck his head in the trailer door. "Get out here and help me. Bring another box of granola bars!"

Odie picked his way across the littered floor to the supply cupboard. He tried to be careful not to step on anything old and precious. He grabbed a fistful of granola bars and made his way back to the door.

"Hurry up, Odie," Kiff called. "I can hear him out there somewhere, chewing."

Kiff was shining his flashlight beam around the clearing, trying to pick up a flash of red dog hair. "There you are," he shot over his shoulder to Odie. "What took you so long?"

"I was trying to clean up some of the mess *you* made!" Odie told him. "Everything's all mixed up in there. You've probably wrecked a whole summer's digging, you know that?"

"Why do you keep saying *I* did it?" Kiff swung the flashlight beam in Odie's face. "It was Drool that knocked over the bins."

"Because you were snooping in them." Odie was mad. "If you'd left them alone, if you hadn't touched that old gun ... "

"While we're standing here arguing, Drool is probably chewing up the bones of an old fur trader!" Kiff said. "Drool! Come on boy, I've got something better than old bones."

They moved cautiously forward in the direction of the chomping sound.

"There!" Kiff's flashlight picked out something moving in the bushes. He focused the beam on the bush and dashed forward. In his mad dash, he tripped over a taut string. The flashlight went flying out of his hand and Kiff felt himself falling forward.

"Odie!" he howled.

"Where are you, Kokatow?" Odie's voice came from somewhere above him.

"I think I've fallen into the old fort. It's wet down here. It's ... horrible." Kiff had a sudden flash of bones sticking out of the damp walls of dirt around him. "Get me out of here!"

"Get yourself out. I'm going after Drool. I can see him, just over there ... " Kiff could see Odie's flashlight beam swinging wildly over the clearing, lighting up a treetop, then the sky.

"Ohhh! Hel-l-l-p!" Kiff heard a sudden cry. The flashlight beam was gone. Everything was darkness.

"Odie?" Kiff called. "What happened? Where are you?"

"The same place you are," came the muffled answer. "Down a hole."

They should have been more careful, Kiff thought. They should have remembered the place was full of excavations. He remembered how it had looked in the dusk — squares marked out with string, with wood stakes in the corners. A maze of deep holes where the workers had been digging.

There was a rustle above his head, and a happy growl, inviting him to play. Drool! Kiff felt something strike him on the head. He bent over and felt in the darkness. His hand jerked back as if it had been burnt. Drool had dropped the slimy ancient bone on his head. If he wasn't going to chase him, the game was no fun.

"This is the last straw, Drool!" Kiff roared. "When I get out of here, I'm going to kill you!"

"Be careful climbing out!" Odie called in the darkness.

"What do you want me to do, jump straight up without touching the sides?" Kiff shouted back. "It's been raining all day. How can you be careful climbing out of a muck hole!"

"But remember, Dee told us they dig a centimetre at a time so they won't disturb anything.

We could be wrecking all that!" Odie's worried voice sounded far away.

"Well, I'm not staying down here!" Kiff started to bellow and then his body was thrown backwards and his mouth was full of fur. "Ooof!" The air was punched out of his lungs as Drool's massive body landed on him, full force.

Kiff felt something in the mud underneath them give way. Help! He was sinking backwards into a deeper hole.

There was the smell of rotten wood and a cracking sound. Kiff struggled frantically to shove Drool off him so he could roll away from the hole.

Drool tried to help by scrambling to his feet, but all he managed to do was push Kiff further in. Kiff grabbed for something, anything in the darkness, but it was too late. His head struck something hard and his shoulder wedged against a solid surface. He was backwards, upside down and stuck, with his feet kicking wildly in the air.

Drool growled and grabbed Kiff's pant leg between his teeth. This was a new kind of game! A person was upside down in a hole, kicking his feet. The dog's job was to catch a foot and hold on. "Rrrrrrr."

"Drool, stop! Odie, help!" Kiff's heart was thumping so hard he could hardly yell. The musty smell was all around him. It was darker than dark.

Odie's answer was faint and far away. "What's happening over there? Don't disturb the arti-facts!"

Don't disturb the artifacts. Don't disturb the artifacts. "I'm *stuck* in an artifact, Od," he hol-lered. "I may be a *permanent part* of this artifact, if you don't get me out!" Kiff was afraid to reach out in the darkness, in case there were more bones. What had he fallen into? He didn't want to think, but it was some kind of a wood box.

A sudden flashlight beam hit his eye then swung away, leaving him blind and blinking for a second. Odie, at last!

"Kiff? Are you down there?"

"Rrrrr" Drool growled in return, lashing Kiff's pant leg back and forth.

"Drool, stop that. Be quiet. Kiff?" Odie's voice was really worried now. "Are you all right?"

Kiff thought briefly about playing dead to get even with Odie, but that would mean staying in this muddy tomb a minute longer than he had to. "I'm as good as I could be, buried alive!" he shouted. "Get down here and get me out!"

"Oh boy," Odie muttered as he lowered himself the two metres into the hole. "Drool, stop. What have you done!"

Drool sat back in the mud and looked interested as Odie hauled Kiff up by the legs. He could have done that — if he'd known *that* was the game. He gave Kiff a friendly lick and slobber as his face emerged. Then he peered down into the hole, sniffing in excitement.

"Give me the flashlight," Kiff said, when he could get his breath. "Get your big head out of the way, Drool! I want to see what's in there."

Kiff was on his hands and knees in the mud. "It's a big rotten old box," he said. "The rain must have washed away the next layer of dirt. Then when Drool jumped on me, the lid just caved in. Wow, Odie, look!"

The box was deep and long. "This could be an important find!" Kiff's voice was hoarse with excitement. "There's something in there."

18

The Spyglass

"Is it a skele-t-ton?" Odie's teeth were chattering.

"I don't know." Kiff was more interested than scared now. "I can see something that looks like cloth, with buttons, and shiny stuff. I wonder what's underneath it?"

"Kiff! Don't touch!" Odie said urgently. "I saw a thing about finding a body frozen in the Alps, and people tried to dig it out because they didn't know it was thousands of years old, and they wrecked it."

"Well, I don't think there's a body in the box, and I've already fallen into it anyway. Ugh! I hope it's not a body." Kiff said. He reached in and gently lifted back a corner of the cloth. There was something long and thin in there.

Kiff felt carefully. His fingers touched something cold and hard. It shone dully in the flashlight beam.

"It's too shiny to be a skeleton. It looks like an old-fashioned pirate's spyglass!" Kiff said, choking with excitement. "Man, this is terrific, Odie."

"You're getting mud on it," Odie pointed out.

"You're right," Kiff lifted a long silver tube gently out of the chest. "We'll have to take good care of this."

Just then Drool gave a low growl in his throat. Kiff had his hand on the dog's neck and could feel the warning vibration. "What's the matter, big guy?" Kiff said.

From the other side of the clearing Efstur suddenly gave a startled whinny. They were listening to something only dogs and horses could hear.

Kiff and Odie, froze, straining for a sound in the darkness. It was long moments before they heard it — a truck motor, approaching slowly over the uneven rock and dirt road.

"Turn off your light!" Kiff said sharply, knowing that in this wilderness darkness any beam of light could be seen for a long distance.

"Maybe it's Josie and the others coming back to get us," Odie said in a low voice.

"Shhh! I don't think so. Listen Odie — " They both listened hard again. "Do you hear any horse van bumping along behind that truck?"

"No, I don't." Odie said, after a pause.

"Well, I don't think Josie would come back without transportation for the horses," Kiff whispered. "And anyway, don't you recognize the sound of that engine?"

Odie nodded in the darkness. The sound was closer now, and definitely one they'd heard before. This time, it really was Stan and Morley's beat up old pickup!

The truck was almost in the clearing. The sound seemed to fill the night air. The engine coughed to a stop and two doors shut.

Drool's throat was still rumbling. He recognized the sounds too. Kiff kept a grip on his muzzle, but he knew if it came to an all-out wrestling match with Drool there was no way he was going to keep him quiet.

Once again flashlight beams crisscrossed against the sky over their heads. Footsteps came nearer.

Kiff and Odie pressed against the side of the excavation, trying to merge into the blackness of the shadow.

The beam of a light flitted over the dig. "Looks like there's nothin' here." Morley said.

"What's all them stakes and string?" Stan's voice came. "They building something out here?"

"Maybe," Morley's voice answered, "but it's a weird-looking foundation, if they are. I didn't think we'd find the horses down here. For the love of Pete, Stan, are we going to look down every road, track, and beaver trail between here and town?" Morley complained.

"If we have to ... " Stan sounded mad and determined. "Them horses didn't let themselves out of the van. There was hoofprints, leading in this direction. Somebody rode them off. And the dog's gone too."

Drool heard the word *dog* and struggled like a wild thing. They were talking about him. Why couldn't he just go and jump on them? Kiff kept his arm wrapped around his neck. Odie leaned with all his force on Drool's rear end. But it was just a matter of time before he gave them away!

"Let's look down by the lake," Stan said, and they heard the steps crunch away.

"Drool! Stop that … " Kiff whispered urgently, as the big dog struggled to go after them.

Suddenly the air was split by Efstur's frightened uproar. He had smelled the men who had forced him into the van. He filled the night with neighs of alarm. Kiff and Odie could hear Stan and Morley thrashing through the brush toward the two horses.

"He's going to hurt Ef!" Kiff cried. "We've got to do something." Just then, Drool exploded out of Kiff's grasp. In a few seconds they could hear Stan's shout of surprise and Morley crying "Down, you red fool of a dog!"

"Come on," Kiff whispered fiercely. "Let's get to the horses and hope Drool keeps them busy until we can untie them."

Odie quickly boosted Kiff out of the hole. Then he grabbed Kiff's hand to haul himself out. They snaked across the clearing, lights out, and worked their way through the trees to Efstur and Smoke.

The frightened horses reared and kicked. Kiff felt for Ef's rope in the darkness. A confused scramble of lights and noise told him Stan and Morley were getting closer. "Hurry," Kiff whispered to Odie. But it was too late. Morley's flashlight caught him in its sudden glare. The bright light blinded him and he threw up his hands to shield his eyes.

"Keep away from our horses!" Kiff shouted. He struck out with the spyglass which he still held in his hand and Morley's flashlight went flying off into the bushes.

"Ouch!" screamed Morley in surprise and fury. "Shine your light over here, Stan. It looks like the big dog isn't the only thing keeping these horses company."

19

A Dreadful Drool

Kiff and Odie froze in the beam of Stan's flashlight. Behind them, Efstur was still stomping
and snorting with anger. He had not forgotten
the way these two had forced him into their
van.

"Keep back," Kiff warned. "He's dangerous!"

Stan actually took a step backwards, away
from Ef's sharp flying hooves. But Morley just
laughed.

"That little pipsqueak of a horse? Dangerous?"
He reached for the spyglass in Kiff's hand. "Why
don't you hand over that thing you hit me with
and I'll settle *him* down fast enough."

"No!" Kiff suddenly threw back his arm and
hurled the spyglass with all his strength into
the darkness. There was a distant splash.

Kiff and Odie glanced at each other in horror.
But the spyglass was better in the lake, Kiff
thought, than used as a club on Efstur. Precious
artifact or not!

"You're really bothering me, you know that!" Morley's scowling features looked evil in the glow of Stan's flashlight. "What should we do with these two, Stan?"

"Get them to help us tie the horses behind the truck," Stan answered. "We should be getting out of here."

Morley glared at Kiff. "I'm dying to throw this one in the lake," he growled. "But you're right. First we should see how useful they can be. Bring the horses over to the clearing," he ordered. "And no more dumb tricks."

Smoke was grateful to feel Odie's familiar hands and nuzzled into his neck as Odie undid the reins that were tied to the tree. Efstur took longer to calm, and shook his frosted mane as if to protest as Kiff led him back to the truck.

"What are you going to do with them?" Kiff demanded.

Stan reached in the open window for the rolled up auction poster behind the seat. He uncurled it and shone the beam on the bottom. "Nine o'clock, she starts," he said.

"Dry up, Stan," Morley growled, grabbing the poster and throwing it back through the truck window.

"You can't sell our horses!" Kiff exploded, throwing himself at Morley in a fury.

"Who said anything about selling them?" Morley shrugged. He gave Kiff a shove and turned away.

Stan caught Morley by the sleeve. "Somebody's coming," he hissed.

They had all been too busy to hear a vehicle coming down the trail. The headlights flashed into the clearing. To Kiff it seemed like all the lights in the world had suddenly switched on.

The workers' truck rattled into the clearing and stopped. Amy, Dee and Josie jumped out of the cab. Neil was close behind.

"It's the *louts*," Dee cried.

"We looked all over town for them. Might have known they'd be here!" Josie glared at Stan and Morley.

Drool came dashing up, out of his mind with joy to see Dee, and have everyone together. He whined and licked and frisked in the middle of them all.

"We heard in the hotel these kids was lost," Morley said. "I guess we found 'em for you."

Kiff and Odie, Josie and Dee stared at each other.

"Guess if there's no reward or nothin' we'll be on our way," Morley went on, reaching for the door handle on his truck.

"Wait a second," Amy said. "These kids have accused you of stealing their horses."

"I don't know how they could say that," Stan said. "Their horses are right here." He shrugged and gestured at Efstur and Smoke.

"But ... " Kiff stammered. Were these two going to get away with this? He could see by the confused looks on Amy and Neil's faces that they didn't know what to believe.

"They had them in a van," Josie insisted. "It's up the road with a broken axle."

"It's too late to go chasing broken-down vans tonight," Neil said. "We've had a really long day, thanks to you kids."

"They're bringing another horse van out from town," Amy explained. "Let's just get you guys home to bed."

"No!" Kiff shouted. "They're liars. They stole the horses and they were going to sell them. I can prove it." He pulled himself up on the door of Stan and Morley's truck, reached through the open window and grabbed the auction poster off the seat.

As quick as he had it, Morley had snatched it out of his hands. "I said that's none of your business," he growled. Twisting the poster into a tight cylinder he tossed it into the dark woods.

Drool raced after it. "Bring it back, Drool," Kiff called. Sure enough, Drool pranced back into the lighted clearing, the cylinder of paper between his teeth.

"Give me that!" Morley hollered, diving for the dog. But Drool had perfected coming close but staying just out of reach. He danced out of Stan's grasp and then Kiff's. He didn't see Morley, with a heavy stick, poised over his head, ready to strike.

"Don't you hit my dog!" Dee flew at Morley, striking his arm so the blow landed far from Drool's skull. Morley raised his hand again to strike at Dee.

For a second, Drool looked puzzled. His ears cocked forward and he tipped his head to one side. Was this a new game the man with the stick wanted to play?

Then Dee screamed.

Drool's ears flattened. The hair rose along the back of his neck. His lips peeled back from long curved teeth.

"Drool!" shouted Dee. "Help!"

In the next instant a huge shape flew past Kiff's head and hurled itself at Morley's chest. He fell backwards, pinned to the ground by four enormous feet and a hundred pounds of red dog. White fangs glittered just above his nose.

"Drool?" Kiff could hardly believe his eyes. Drool the fool had become Drool the fierce beast.

"Get him off me, get him off me," Morley babbled. "He's a killer!"

There was no doubt Drool meant business. The hair stuck up all along his spine, making him look twice as large. His nose was wrinkled into a snarl, and the sounds coming from his throat were not friendly.

"Wow!" Kiff gasped to Dee. "He saw you in trouble and he just ... transformed."

Dee grinned. "I always knew he would," she said.

"I guess we should get him off," Odie said, "before he does kill Morley."

"Wait a minute," Dee said. "Before I call off my dog, I'd just like you to tell us what you were going to do with the horses."

"S-Sell'em," Stan stuttered. "They was going to give us $10,000 for the little one."

"It's right here," Kiff picked up the somewhat chewed and slobbered poster from the ground and unrolled it. "The auction's in Tackle Bay tomorrow. The figure and a phone number are written right here."

"Now let me up," Morley moaned. "Call off this monster. Somebody call him off."

"I think we'll just leave Drool on guard till more help arrives." Amy said.

"Stay, Drool," Dee commanded.

Drool sat back, proudly on guard. This man who had threatened Dee wasn't going to move until Dee said it was okay. All in all, it had been a fine day.

20

Kiff's Crimes

"I take back everything I ever said about you, Drool," Kiff said.

Drool was lying blissfully on the ground, his big head resting lovingly on Kiff's knee. His floppy lips made two soft furry puddles on either side of his nose. "Can you believe this dog is the dreaded Drool of last night?" Kiff laughed.

Odie was sitting beside Kiff at the campfire ring at Fort James. "Yeah, Drool was great," Odie sighed. "And Stan and Morley have been charged with horse theft and will probably go to jail — and we'll probably join them."

"What are you talking about?" Kiff stroked Drool's silky red ear.

"I've been making a list of our crimes," Odie said. He showed Kiff his notebook, in which he'd been writing a list.

1. We broke into the supply trailer

2. We spilled the bins and mixed up all the artifacts

3. We collapsed the lid of the old chest and removed the spyglass

4. The spyglass ended up in the lake.

"Wait a second," Kiff said. "All of those crimes are mine. I did all that stuff!"

"I know," Odie sighed again. "But I'll get blamed, so I might as well admit to it. We are in *so* much trouble."

The Fort James archaeological team had listened to Kiff's story, and this morning were looking into the discovery of the chest. They had made a sort of tent over that part of the excavation so that no more rain or debris could fall into the hole. They had told Kiff and the others to keep out of their way while they worked.

"What about the spyglass?" Kiff said. "If they find that, and it is important, they'll forget about the rest." He sighed again. "I wish they'd let us dive for it," Kiff said. "We know where it went down."

"No, we don't," Odie said. "It was dark, remember? Anyway, they're afraid you'll muck up the bottom." Two workers were out in a boat, going slowly back and forth, searching for the spyglass.

"Well," Kiff said. "I wanted to spend the week before school out in the woods, and it looks like I will be. I just wish they'd give us something to do!" Everyone was so busy. Even Josie and Dee had a job straightening up the trailer. The boys had just been told to stay out of the way and keep Drool from driving everyone crazy.

"Anyway, I've figured out the fort," Kiff said. "Those two holes we fell in last night used to be buildings. They called them *bastions*, and they had them at all four corners. Then there was a sort of building in the middle, and a log palisade, like a wall, around the whole thing. I can just picture it." Kiff squinted his eyes and looked out over the lake. The sun was sparkling on calm water and in his imagination he could see loaded freight canoes paddling towards the fort.

Just then, there was a cry from the boat on the lake. One of the workers held up a long thin object and shouted.

Drool leaped to his feet, in one second transformed from a peacefully sleeping bag of bones to a huge engine of energy. "No, Drool," Kiff laughed, "It is not a stick. That's our spyglass."

Kiff and Odie raced down to the shore where an excited cluster of workers was already gathering. The young man who had found it was wading ashore, too excited to care if his shoes or pant legs were soaked. He was holding the spyglass over his head like a trophy.

This, of course, drove Drool mad. He was sure the young man was going to throw that stick for him. He pranced into the water, tail held high.

"Help me get him, Odie," Kiff cried. This was their last chance. If Drool grabbed that spyglass and ran off with it, they would never be forgiven!

They dived at Drool from opposite sides, just as he made a leap for the young man with the spyglass. Kiff and Odie landed on their faces in the shallow water with a mighty splash. They heard laughter from the shore.

"Nice try, guys. Come on Drool, here's a better stick." It was Dee with a nice, thick rawhide chew stick in her hand.

As far as Drool was concerned, this was the best stick of all. He wheeled around and bounded up to Dee, who slid his choke collar over his head with the leash attached while he happily fastened his huge teeth on the rawhide.

"Thanks, Dee." Kiff waded ashore, dripping. "Where were you with the rawhide a minute ago?"

Meanwhile the discoverers of the spyglass were surrounded by a tight knot of archaeology students and workers. Josie had run down from the trailer to join them. Now she dashed over to give them the news.

"It's got an inscription," she said in excitement. "It belonged to Chevalier de Troyes. He explored up here in the 1600s. That's three hundred years ago! They're flipping out over there!"

"Maybe everything in the chest belonged to him," Kiff said. "Wow, and I fell right into it."

Josie laughed. "That's the only way you ever do anything, Kokatow," she said. "But I'm glad you did if it means Dee can come back for another summer with her family."

* * *

That night there was a huge celebration around the campfire. A huge pot of fresh vegetarian chili was cooked over the open fire. Big slabs of toast and endless marshmallows were roasted over the coals.

Kiff and Odie, Josie and Dee stayed to finish the bag of marshmallows. "Did you ever notice," Dee said, "how older people only eat one or two?" They all nodded at the strange truth of this.

"Did you realize," Kiff told the others, "that this is what the fur traders ate on their huge canoe trips? Beans and bread."

"Maybe not marshmallows," Odie said. He liked to toast his marshmallows nice and slow, until they were golden all around and gooey in the middle.

"And did you know you could put your canoe in the water right down there," Kiff pointed at the lake with his marshmallow stick, "and paddle to Montreal?"

"To New York City," Josie said. "My dad says he knew an old man who did it. Paddled all the way to Montreal, and then down through

Lake Champlain and the Hudson River to the docks of New York."

"Could you still do that?" Kiff jumped up. His marshmallow was on fire and he blew on it to put out the flame.

"I guess so. You'd have to portage over some new hydro dams, but sure ... the rivers and lakes are still there."

"Then let's do it. Next summer. What do you say?"

"Without Drool," Odie said.

As usual, Drool, who had been sleeping peacefully with his nose to the fire, leaped to his feet when he heard his name. His big red plume of a tail swished through the air, connecting with Kiff's charred and oozing marshmallow just as it slid off the stick.

"Stand back!" Kiff shouted. "Marshmallow tail on the loose!"

Drool raced around the group as they tried to scuttle away. In seconds they had streamers of melted marshmallow on their sleeves, on their faces, in their hair. "Yuck," Dee groaned as she peeled away the goo, but Drool made happy sounds as he licked their sticky faces.

"I don't know," Josie laughed. "What would life be without a little Drool?"

Afterword

Fort James is an imaginary fur-trading post, based on a real post called Fort Matachewan. It was one of the furthest-flung outposts of the Northwest Company, based in Montreal. Voyageurs paddled large birchbark canoes to the main post at the head of Lake Timiskaming. From there traders would work their way up a chain of smaller lakes and rivers to posts such as Fort Matachewan. When they had to portage around rapids and waterfalls, they carried packs and canoes over trails first made by animals, later followed by generations of Native People. Many of these portages are still used by canoeists today, but the old forts are only memories. If you found the ruins of such a place, you might find a medallion with a picture of a beaver — the emblem of the Northwest fur traders.